CLEVER BRIDGE TRICKS

Clever Bridge Tricks

BRIAN SENIOR

faber and faber

LONDON · BOSTON

First published in 1988
by Faber and Faber Limited
3 Queen Square London WC1N 3AU

Typeset by Goodfellow and Egan Ltd Cambridge
Printed in England by Clays Ltd, St Ives plc

ISBN 0-571-14919-7

A CIP record for this book is
available from the British Library

2 4 6 8 10 9 7 5 3

Contents

Foreword

The main thing that sets the expert apart from the average player is his *tactical* approach to the play of a hand. His technique, in the form of making difficult plays, may not be much different from that of other players, but allied to technique is the art of deception to create a false picture in the mind of an opponent. Quite apart from deep strategical plans, there is a right and a wrong way of playing almost every suit combination.

There is no reason why deception should be the weapon of the expert only; or rather, anyone can become an expert in this area of the game with a little effort. My aim has been to cover a variety of false-carding situations and to help you to develop the necessary flexibility of mind. To find the correct solutions to a number of problems you will need to use your imagination, to get inside your opponent's head. You will soon begin to recognize situations in actual play where the use of deception might be appropriate. You will acquire the reputation of being a difficult person to play against – an expert declarer and a tricky defender. Good luck!

Brian Senior

1

Attracting a continuation

If complex squeezes and elimination plays are the science of declarer play, then surely deception – painting a false picture of your hand to fox the defence – is its art. Merely knowing the techniques involved is not sufficient, you also have to know when and how to use them. Your play may well be affected by your assessment of the opposition. It is no use playing a delicate false card against a defender who never bothers to watch the spot cards; this is indeed casting pearls before swine. Equally, however, an expert may be alerted that something funny is going on if you false-card too obviously – the sort of play necessary against the tyro.

There are many different types of deception, depending partly on your estimate of your opponent. Sometimes the simple choice of a spot card when following suit may be all that is required, while on other occasions you may have to build up a false picture in a defender's mind by your play in three suits so as to enlist his aid in playing the fourth successfully.

Perhaps the best known type of deception is the false card on the opening lead, the aim being to confuse the opposition's signals so that they are uncertain whether or not to continue to attack the same suit. It is also a situation where deception is abused due to an insufficient understanding of the principles involved. Without realizing it, players often make life easier for the defence rather than more difficult.

There are any number of situations in which you might wish to persuade the defence to continue to attack a suit. Take this example:

♠ J 10 5	♠ 7 6 3 2
♡ A K Q	♡ J 9 8
◇ A Q 6 3 2	◇ K 5 4
♣ Q 10	♣ 8 5 3

You opened 1NT (16–18) and everyone passed. The opening lead is the jack of diamonds, on which South plays the 7. How should you proceed?

Clearly you will have no problem if diamonds are 3–2 as you will be able to take the first eight tricks. Suppose however that they are 4–1, quite likely in view of the lead. Now if you win the first trick and play three more rounds of the suit to set up the long card North should have little difficulty in finding the killing switch. You will lose at least four clubs, three spades and one diamond, ending up two or more down.

The key to success is to appreciate that you do not actually need five diamond tricks for your contract; four will do. If you duck the opening lead in both hands you give up the chance of an overtrick but almost guarantee the contract as North will almost certainly continue diamonds. Just to make even more certain, drop the 6 from your hand as it will now appear that South has started an echo from something like Q 7 3 2 to encourage a continuation. The time to force North to make a decision is now when he knows very little about the hand. Had you won the first diamond and returned the suit, he would have seen you turn up with A Q to five and also observed his partner's discards.

The hand illustrates two of the important principles of deception. First, the earlier you put a defender to the test the tougher is his problem as he has less to go on. Second, when following with small cards declarer should generally 'signal' as if he were a defender. In other words, play a low card to try to discourage a continuation, a high card to encourage. Sometimes it will be very difficult for the leader to tell who is doing the signalling.

On the following hand you want to see your right-hand opponent continue the suit led.

♠ A Q 10   ♠ K J 8 4
♡ A 4   ♡ 7 6 3
♢ A 8 7   ♢ K J 6 4
♣ Q 10 9 3 2   ♣ J 8

You are in 3NT and North leads ♣ 4 to his partner's ace. A heart switch could be extremely dangerous, so you would very much like to see South return his partner's suit. If you play small under the ace, South will know that you have at least a four-card suit and may see no future in clubs. Correct play is to drop the 9 as it may well look to South as though the lead was from a six-card suit; in this case he will surely continue, giving you the tempo you need.

Opportunity for this type of false-carding is by no means restricted to play in notrumps. Take the situation where an ace is led against a suit contract and you hold something like Q 8 2 opposite dummy's 7 5 3. If right-hand opponent follows with the 4, you know that he doesn't want a continuation, but you do as it is your only chance of making the queen. Try the effect of dropping the 8. Left-hand opponent may well assume his partner to have started an echo. Whether he is showing the queen or merely an even number it will be safe to continue. From his point of view the position could be any of the following:

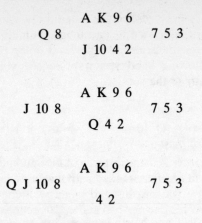

```
        A K 9 6
Q 8                7 5 3
        J 10 4 2


        A K 9 6
J 10 8             7 5 3
        Q 4 2


        A K 9 6
Q J 10 8           7 5 3
        4 2
```

In all these cases a continuation will be good for the defence; it is only when West holds Q 8 2 that it will cost a trick.

Sometimes you may have no positive desire for a continuation but you will want to avoid a potentially devastating switch. For example, North leads the 10 and your holding is Q 8 6 2 opposite A K J. Obviously you cannot gain a trick in this suit, but it can hardly hurt to have the defence continue to attack it. Go up with the ace and drop the 6 from your own hand. It may look to North as though he has found partner's suit, in which case he will lead it again when he has the chance.

As declarer, you must beware of false-carding just for the sake of it as sometimes a thoughtless false card may actually help the defence – the last thing you want. For example, North, who has overcalled in spades, leads the ace of spades against your 4 ♡ contract and this is the spade suit:

```
        A K J 9 7
5 2                Q 8 3
        10 6 4
```

4

Here, to play the 5 from hand is quite OK as you are very happy to see a spade continuation. Change the position to:

A K J 9 7

10 6 5 2   Q 8 3

4

and now you should play the 2. North may not be able to tell whether his partner has one or three of the suit and may switch. If, however, you had false-carded with the 5 or 6 he would have noted that the 2 was missing and might well continue on the assumption that his partner had started an echo with 4 2.

The position is much the same when a suit is distributed like this:

A K 9 6 5

J 8 3   Q 10 7

4 2

If the ace is led to the 7 and 4, all a false card of the 8 does is emphasize South's echo; the 4 may not look much with only the 2 missing, but if both the 2 and 3 are missing, that is a different matter.

It is essential to think before false-carding. Be sure that the card you choose actually helps your cause, not the opponents'. As a rule, if you want to encourage, play the card above that of your right-hand opponent. Equally important, do your thinking before playing from dummy; if you have to think after everyone else has played to the trick the opposition will view any card you play with considerable suspicion.

Another way in which to attract a continuation is by the unnecessary play of an honour card to feign shortage in the suit led. Take this example:

♠ A Q 10   ♠ J 9 7 3
♡ 9 8 6   ♡ J 7 4
♢ A K 5   ♢ J 10 6
♣ K J 9 4   ♣ A Q 6

North leads a low diamond against your 3NT and naturally enough you play the jack. Suppose that when South plays low you allow the jack to hold and take a losing spade finesse. North will know there is no future in diamonds and is all too likely to find the killing heart switch. Better to overtake dummy's jack with your king, cross to dummy in clubs, and take the spade finesse. Perhaps North should still get the position right, but he may be tempted to continue diamonds, thinking you have A K bare.

Similar plays may well prove effective with other honour combinations, such as:

(1) K 10 5 opposite J 9 7

(2) A J 4 opposite Q 10

(3) A Q 9 opposite J 10 5

In each case North leads a low card, you play high from dummy, and South follows with a small card.

If in (1) and (2) you underplay the 10 and jack respectively, and in (3) overtake with the queen, you may persuade North that you started with a doubleton and that he can lead the suit a second time. In (2) you will gain a tempo, while in (1) and (3) you will also gain a trick.

There is sometimes scope for even more spectacular play:

♠ K J 7 4   ♠ A Q 5
♡ Q 3   ♡ 9 7 2
♢ A Q 8   ♢ 9 4
♣ A 9 6 3   ♣ Q J 10 8 7

You are in 3NT and North leads a low diamond to his partner's jack. The natural play is to win the queen, cross to dummy and take the club finesse. The drawback to this line is that you have pinpointed the heart switch, and if the finesse fails any competent defender will defeat you. But suppose you win the *ace* at trick one. When the club finesse loses, will not North continue with another low diamond to his partner's queen? It is true that with A x x of diamonds you might have ducked the first two tricks, but on the other hand if he thinks about it at all he will probably just decide that you did not bother because the critical finesse had to be taken into the danger hand anyway. As with the previous examples, you did not need the extra trick so could afford to sacrifice it, at least temporarily, to improve the chance of a defensive error.

The same idea should work with, say, K J x x opposite dummy's small singleton. If the opening lead is a small card to South's 10 and you are afraid of a switch to another suit, try winning with the king! Surely North will underlead his A Q again when he has the chance; it will look to him as though the opening lead has struck gold.

Even when you are not trying anything really spectacular it is important to win with the right honour if you have a choice.

Take this hand:

♠ A J 10 4	♠ Q 7 3
♡ A K Q	♡ 8 6 2
◇ Q 10 4	◇ K J 9 5
♣ 7 4 2	♣ A 8 6

As before, you are in 3NT and North leads the jack of
hearts. How many times have I seen declarer win with the ace
from such a holding, thinking no doubt that he was being
clever! Far from being devious, the play of the ace merely
serves to emphasize the true position, making a switch all too
likely. If you win with the queen, North can be fairly sure that
you have A K Q but South may hope that his partner has
either A J 10 or K J 10. Winning the king on the other hand
leaves South with only one hope – A J 10 – as he knows you
have the queen from his partner's lead, but it leaves North with
the hope of finding his partner with the queen. As a rule, the
king is best.

Usually, when you have a choice of two touching honours
with which to win and you would like left-hand opponent to
lead the suit again, you should win with the higher card. For
example, holding A Q J you should win the queen after a low
card has gone to the 10, leaving open the possibility that South
has J 10. However there is an exception. Say you hold A K 10
and the opening lead is low to the queen. Most players would
win with the ace, but in fact the king is better. The reason is that
it is unusual for declarer to win an unsupported ace immediately, so you will be suspected of also holding the king. If you
win with the king, however, you leave open the distinct possibility that South has played the queen from A Q x, frequently
correct play to keep defensive communications fluid.

I stated earlier that a sound general principle was for declarer
to signal as though he were a defender, i.e. play a high card to
encourage a continuation, and low for a switch. This is correct,

but it is important to check on your opponents' system, as not everyone uses traditional signalling methods these days. If opponents play 'reverse signals', such as the 2 to encourage from K 8 2, the 7 to discourage from 7 4 3, you will need to reverse your normal play as declarer.

Another quite common agreement relates to honour leads. Many partnerships have an agreement that against a notrump contract the lead of a 10 promises a higher honour while the jack denies a higher card. It is important to realize that the lead of the 10 or jack therefore automatically cuts out a number of possible holdings from the opening leader's hand. There is clearly no point in trying to create a false picture if your intended victim already knows that it is an impossible one. To return to the problem of which honour to win with from A K Q when left-hand opponent has led the jack, if that jack denies a higher honour then the right hand opponent already knows the true position and cannot be fooled. Any deception therefore has to be aimed at his partner, and winning with the king is probably best as it conceals the position of the queen; even of the ace, because a defender who holds the ace will not always part with it when he knows his partner is jack high.

2

When you want a switch

I have already discussed the correct handling of small cards when you want opponents to switch. There are also several tricks you can try with honour cards.

Except against a very strong opponent, if you have a choice of honours with which to win a trick you should usually win with the lower one. For example, dummy has only small cards and the opening lead is low to the jack. Holding K Q bare you should win with the queen, announcing to left-hand opponent that you still have the king as a second stopper. This may well persuade him not to continue the suit when he comes in. Of course, if you want him to continue the suit, say you hold K Q x, you play the higher honour to tempt him and, who knows, you may end up with a second trick.

A very strong player might wonder why you were winning with the queen, making him a present of the fact that you also have the king, when you could have played the king and left him guessing. Assuming that he knows you to be a competent player, he may well draw the correct conclusion, i.e. you are trying to appear strong in the suit because you are actually weak. In that case he may lay down his ace and drop your king. This raises the intriguing thought that perhaps you should win with the king after all and play the queen from K Q x when you do want a continuation – a case of bluff and double bluff.

Many deceptive plays revolve around the principle of playing the card you are known to hold. In each of the following examples you suspect that the lead is from a short suit. What is the best play to avoid the impending ruff?

(1) K Q 10   8 6 5 4   North leads the jack to South's ace.

(2) Q J 10   K 8 6 3   North leads the 2 to the 3 and ace.

(3) J 10 9   K 8 3 2   North leads the 4 to the 2 and queen.

(4) K J 9   7 6 5 3   North leads the 10 to the 3 and ace.

In (1) North's lead denies possession of the queen so that is the card you must play, making it look as though North has the 10 and therefore cannot ruff the second round.

In (2) and (3) you can be fairly certain that the lead is a singleton as North has led the smallest missing card in the suit yet is known to have no honour in it. Your correct play is the middle card – the jack in (2) and the 10 in (3). This leaves open the possibility that it is you who hold the singleton and that North has led from Q 10 2 and J 9 4 respectively. This is your only chance as South will be aware that his partner would not lead small from Q J 2, J 10 2, J 10 4, or 10 9 4.

Again, in (4), you should drop the jack, the card that North has denied, leaving open the possibility that you began with K J bare.

Sometimes you cannot be sure that the lead is from a short suit, but you should false-card anyway just in case.

♠ A Q J 9 7 6 4 3   ♠ K 8
♡ A 7   ♡ K Q 5 2
♢ —   ♢ J 8
♣ K Q 5   ♣ 8 7 6 4 3

Against your excellent contract of 6♠, North leads the 2 of clubs to his partner's ace. You cannot be sure about the lead. It could be from J 9 2, for example, in which case there is no problem, but if it is a singleton you had better do something to divert South from giving his partner a ruff. If you drop either the king or the queen under the ace you have a fair chance of success, as that would be entirely consistent with the lead being from three to an honour. From South's point of view a diamond switch may look quite attractive. True, he is insulting your bidding (as if you would bid a slam missing two aces!), but I think you could live with such a profitable insult, don't you?

Even more likely of success is the correct play on this deal:

```
                    ♠ 10 9
                    ♡ 9 8 5 2
                    ◇ A 10
                    ♣ Q 9 8 5 4
  ♠ K Q J                          ♠ 7 6 5
  ♡ A 4                            ♡ K Q 7
  ◇ K Q 8 7 3 2                    ◇ J 9 5 4
  ♣ K 6                            ♣ J 7 3
                    ♠ A 8 4 3 2
                    ♡ J 10 6 3
                    ◇ 6
                    ♣ A 10 2
```

West	East
1◇	2◇
3NT	Pass

North leads the 5 of clubs to South's ace. If you woodenly play low, South will no doubt continue clubs, playing his partner for honour to five. It looks rather spectacular, but what is South to think if you smoothly drop the king under his ace? He knows that the king is not singleton so will surely credit you with the queen. Suspecting your long diamond suit from the bidding, he is very likely to switch to spades, thinking that the clubs would be set up too late to do the defence any good.

There are other situations where it can hardly cost to drop an unnecessary honour, particularly after an opposing pre-emptive bid.

K 6   10 7 4

This is the heart suit and you are in 4♠ after South opened 3♡. If North leads the queen to South's ace it can hardly cost to drop the king. Rather than risk setting up dummy's 10 South will nearly always switch. Even if at this stage you have no obvious parking place for the heart loser the play is still correct as something may develop later that is to your advantage. Both defenders will be playing under the misapprehension that you started life with the bare king and might form a wrong picture of the rest of the hand.

It is the same when you have K x opposite J x x of a suit in which an opponent pre-empted. It doesn't matter which defender has ace queen to seven; if you play the king under his ace he will be extremely loth to continue the suit – after all, dummy's jack could be your game-going trick.

Most deception revolving around the play of honours involves the play of an unnecessarily high card to conceal your actual strength or weakness. But there are also what might be called positional plays such as:

K 4   Q 10 3

When North leads the 9 against your notrump contract it is clear that he has found a dangerous attack. Your king is about to be knocked out at trick one, and when North regains the lead his partner will be poised with such as A J x x over dummy's Q 10. There is no genuine chance, but there is an excellent psychological one. Suppose your actual holding was K x x; then your correct play would be to rise with dummy's queen at trick one, since if South wins with his ace he cannot profitably continue the suit. You know that you don't have the third card in your hand, but South doesn't, so try the same play of the

13

queen, anyway. Unless he is of a highly suspicious nature South will probably switch and give you a vital tempo.

The same type of play gives an extra chance on this deal:

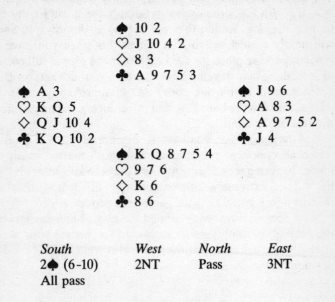

South	West	North	East
2♠ (6-10)	2NT	Pass	3NT
All pass			

North leads the 10 of spades.

If the diamond finesse is successful the contract will always be made and your play to trick one will matter little. What if the finesse fails?

Suppose the play to trick one goes 10, jack, queen, ace, and you take a losing diamond finesse. South can put his partner in with the ace of clubs for a spade lead through dummy's 9, putting you three down. The play with the best chance of success is to cover the 10 with the jack and let South's queen hold the trick. South may think that you have the missing small spade, in which case leading a second round up to dummy's 9 is just giving you a free trick. Particularly at match-pointed pairs he will not wish to risk that and may switch.

As always, the key to a play of this kind is to put yourself in the defender's position. Think what holding he might be afraid of, then try to convince him that this is your actual holding. You know the truth, but he doesn't. Much of the time he will be guessing, and nobody guesses right all the time.

These problems have no relation to the surrounding text. They are in no particular order and are of varying difficulty, just as you would find in real life. Don't worry if you don't solve them all correctly first time round; the main thing is to grasp the principles involved.

Question No 1

Dealer West   Love all

♠ K Q 7 4
♡ K 9 6 2
♢ 10 4
♣ J 7 2

♣ A led

♠ J 10 9 8 2
♡ A Q 10
♢ Q 7 3
♣ Q 6

The bidding

South	West	North	East
—	1 ♣	Pass	1 ♢
Pass	1NT	Pass	2 ♣
2 ♠ [1]	Pass	Pass	3 ♣
Pass	Pass	3 ♠	Pass
Pass	Pass		

Final contract – Three Spades

[1] Since both opponents are now limited it is reasonably safe for South to contest the part score.

The early play

West begins with ace, king and a third club.

Preliminary analysis

The defenders have not, so far, taken their five top tricks, but of course they will soon come in again with the ace of trumps. Is there any way in which you may deter them from promptly putting you one down?

```
                    ♠ K Q 7 4
                    ♡ K 9 6 2
                    ◇ 10 4
                    ♣ J 7 2
 ♠ A 6                              ♠ 5 3
 ♡ 8 7 5 3                          ♡ J 4
 ◇ K 9 6                            ◇ A J 8 5 2
 ♣ A K 9 4                          ♣ 10 8 5 3
                    ♠ J 10 9 8 2
                    ♡ A Q 10
                    ◇ Q 7 3
                    ♣ Q 6
```

South	West	North	East
—	1 ♣	Pass	1 ◇
Pass	1NT	Pass	2 ♣
2 ♠	Pass	Pass	3 ♣
Pass	Pass	3 ♠	Pass
Pass	Pass		

West begins with three rounds of clubs.

You have been lucky so far in avoiding a diamond switch, but if you discard a diamond now and play on trumps you can hardly expect your luck to hold. Try pitching the 10 of hearts instead and then playing spades. Many players in West's position would dart in with the ace of spades and lead a heart. Silly, of course, because if the declarer has heart losers he will not be able to dispose of them.

It would be slightly risky for West to take the ace of spades on the second round and then lead a diamond, because East's high cards might be in hearts and not in the suit he has bid. No defence on the West hand is completely safe.

Question No 2

Dealer South   Game all

```
                    ♠ K 10 9
                    ♡ 8 7 4
                    ◇ A Q 4 2
                    ♣ A 3 2
      ♠ 6 led
                    ♠ A Q J 8 7
                    ♡ Q 9
                    ◇ K 8
                    ♣ K Q 7 6
```

The bidding

South	West	North	East
1 ♠	Pass	2 ◇	Pass
3NT[1]	Pass	4NT[2]	Pass
6NT[3]	Pass	Pass	Pass

Final contract – 6NT

[1] Not everyone's choice – but Q x is usually a good holding for declarer in a notrump contract.
[2] Natural, since it is a raise of notrumps.
[3] 'I never refuse an invitation,' said South later.

The early play

West led a low spade – and East showed out, discarding a low heart.

Preliminary analysis

You have escaped a heart lead, but there are only eleven tricks on top. The clubs could be 3–3, but it's very unlikely since the spades are 5–0; also, East has discarded a heart, not a club, on the first trick.

21

```
                        ♠ K 10 9
                        ♡ 8 7 4
                        ◇ A Q 4 2
                        ♣ A 3 2
      ♠ 6 5 4 3 2                        ♠ —
      ♡ A 10 6                           ♡ K J 5 3 2
      ◇ J 7 3                            ◇ 10 9 6 5
      ♣ 8 5                              ♣ J 10 9 4
                        ♠ A Q J 8 7
                        ♡ Q 9
                        ◇ K 8
                        ♣ K Q 7 6
```

South	West	North	East
1 ♠	Pass	2 ◇	Pass
3NT	Pass	4NT	Pass
6NT	Pass	Pass	Pass

West leads a spade and East discards a low heart.

You have eleven tricks on top and the chance of the clubs breaking 3–3 is extremely slim. One possibility is to run five spade tricks, putting East under some pressure. The weakness of this line is that West will have an easy opportunity to play spades from the top, indicating to his partner that he, West, can look after the high suit, hearts

Certainly it would not be bad play to cash the spades, but a different line is more likely to succeed. What about a heart to the queen at trick two? Madness? No, not at all. So long as East does not hold A K and West does not hold such as A J 10 or K J 10, the odds are that West will win but will not return the suit. (He may even hold off the queen!) If West takes the ace of hearts and returns a different suit, the chance of a squeeze against East will be very good indeed. As the cards lie, East will be squeezed in the minors.

Question No 3

Dealer South   Love all

                ♠ K 7 3
                ♡ 5 2
                ♢ Q 9 5 4
                ♣ J 7 5 4

♢ 2 led

                ♠ Q
                ♡ A Q J 9 6 3
                ♢ A
                ♣ A K Q 10 2

The bidding

South	West	North	East
2 ♡[1]	Pass	2NT	Pass
3 ♣	Pass	4 ♣	Pass
6 ♣[2]	Pass	Pass	Pass

Final contract – Six Clubs

[1] Strong enough for Two Clubs, but on two-suiters an Acol Two Bid is often a better choice.
[2] Partner is unlikely to hold all the cards necessary for a grand slam. The small slam is likely to depend on the heart finesse at worst.

The early play

West led the 2 of diamonds.

Preliminary analysis

The contract appears to depend on the heart finesse, as you expected. Is there any way to improve your chances?

♠ K 7 3
♡ 5 2
♢ Q 9 5 4
♣ J 7 5 4

♠ J 8 5 4   ♠ A 10 9 6 2
♡ K 8   ♡ 10 7 4
♢ 10 7 3 2   ♢ K J 8 6
♣ 9 8 3   ♣ 6

♠ Q
♡ A Q J 9 6 3
♢ A
♣ A K Q 10 2

South	West	North	East
2 ♡	Pass	2NT	Pass
3 ♣	Pass	4 ♣	Pass
6 ♣	Pass	Pass	Pass

West leads the 2 of diamonds. South can do slightly better than rest his entire fortune on the heart finesse. He plays the *queen* of diamonds from dummy at trick one, covers the king with the ace, and leads a club to dummy's jack. Then he finesses the queen of hearts. It is surely possible now that West, instead of switching to spades, will play another diamond. Note that this play of the heart finesse should be made early on: don't give East a chance to signal on the second round of trumps

This play of the queen of diamonds had something of a vogue about fifteen years ago, and you may have seen it before. There are other deceptions of the same kind when you want to give defenders the impression that they have found your weakness. For example, you may play dummy's jack from J x x in front of your own doubleton A K or A Q.

Question No 4

Dealer West   N–S vulnerable

                     ♠ 6 5
                     ♡ J 10 5
                     ◇ K Q 9 8 6 2
                     ♣ 6 2
    ♡ 9 led

                     ♠ Q J 9 7 2
                     ♡ A 4
                     ◇ A 10 3
                     ♣ A Q J

The bidding

South	West	North	East
—	1 ♣	Pass	1 ♡
dble	Pass	3 ◇¹	Pass
3NT	Pass	Pass	Pass

Final contract – 3NT

¹ A bit pushy, do you think? Not at all, when partner doubles after both opponents have bid.

The early play

West leads the 9 of hearts. You cover with the 10 and East plays the queen.

Preliminary analysis

This contract should be fairly safe if the hearts are 6–2, but suppose they are 5–3. Even if your opponents normally lead low from three small, West would probably have led the 9 from 9 8 3. If that is the case, what is your best chance?

♠ 6 5
♥ J 10 5
♦ K Q 9 8 6 2
♣ 6 2

♠ A K 4
♥ 9 8 3
♦ J 4
♣ K 10 7 4 3

♠ 10 8 3
♥ K Q 7 6 2
♦ 7 5
♣ 9 8 5

♠ Q J 9 7 2
♥ A 4
♦ A 10 3
♣ A Q J

South	West	North	East
—	1 ♣	Pass	1 ♥
dble	Pass	3 ♦	Pass
3NT	Pass	Pass	Pass

West's lead of the 9 of hearts is covered by the 10 and queen.

At the table South took the ace of hearts and cashed six diamonds. West was not particularly embarrassed – he can even afford a high spade.

'Perhaps I ought to have held up the ace of hearts in case East held six,' South remarked to his partner. 'As they are 5–3 it wouldn't have helped.'

But it might well have done! If South plays smoothly low on the first trick, East may think he holds A x x and may switch to a club, which leaves the declarer with no problem at all (barring a possible 4–0 break in diamonds). And the contract will always be safe if the hearts are 6–2, since East can hardly have an entry.

Quite right; the deal is similar to that of the deal on page 14. I wanted to make sure you were learning!

Question No 5

Dealer North   N–S vulnerable

```
              ♠ A J 9 3
              ♡ 10 5
              ♢ A 9
              ♣ A K Q 5 4
  ♠ K led
              ♠ 6 2
              ♡ A K Q J 9 8
              ♢ Q 10 5 4
              ♣ 7
```

The bidding

South	West	North	East
—	—	1 ♣	Pass
4 ♡[1]	Pass	4NT	Pass
5 ♡[2]	Pass	7 ♡[3]	Pass
Pass	Pass		

Final contract – Seven Hearts

[1] 'To shut out the spades,' he explained afterwards.

[2] Showing one ace and a critical king, which in this case would be in one of the bid suits.

[3] It looks as though there will be at least twelve tricks on top, with good chances for a thirteenth.

The early play

West leads the king of spades. South wins in dummy – that can't be wrong, anyway.

Preliminary analysis

There seem to be only eleven tricks on top. A 4–3 break in clubs would produce a twelfth, but where will the thirteenth come from?

```
              ♠ A J 9 3
              ♡ 10 5
              ◇ A 9
              ♣ A K Q 5 4
♠ K Q 10 4                    ♠ 8 7 5
♡ 6 4                         ♡ 7 3 2
◇ K 8 7 2                     ◇ J 6 3
♣ J 8 3                       ♣ 10 9 6 2
              ♠ 6 2
              ♡ A K Q J 9 8
              ◇ Q 10 5 4
              ♣ 7
```

South	West	North	East
—	—	1 ♣	Pass
4 ♡	Pass	4NT	Pass
5 ♡	Pass	7 ♡	Pass
Pass	Pass		

When West leads the king of spades, prospects are poor. There are one or two genuine chances, but they are very faint. For example, a singleton king of diamonds in the West hand would carry you a long way.

Undoubtedly the best plan is to assume that West has the king of diamonds and play on his nerves. Win with the ace of spades, lead a heart to the ace, and advance the queen of diamonds. Would West cover? He might not. If the queen of diamonds holds you mustn't play a second round: you must draw trumps and trust to the clubs breaking 4–3.

If the queen of diamonds is covered by the king you need not despair altogether. If West began with K Q 10 of spades, K J of diamonds, and four clubs, he will have a difficult time when you play five more rounds of hearts.

Question No 6

Dealer North   Game all

♠ J 10 2
♡ A Q 6 2
♢ K
♣ K J 7 6 2

♢ 10 led

♠ A 8 4 3
♡ K 5 3
♢ A J 3
♣ 10 9 4

The bidding

South	West	North	East
—	—	1 ♣	Pass
2NT[1]	Pass	3NT[2]	Pass
Pass	Pass		

Final contract – 3NT

[1] The game is littered with players who make it a 'rule' to respond in a 4-card major at the one level. Let's leave them to it.

[2] It is *just* possible that four hearts would be a better contract, but most unlikely. In general, it is a mistake to present opponents with added information.

The early play

West begins with the 10 of diamonds, won by dummy's king, East playing the 5.

Preliminary analysis

You need to establish your clubs, obviously, before the defenders can run tricks in diamonds.

Answer No 6

```
                    ♠ J 10 2
                    ♡ A Q 6 2
                    ◇ K
                    ♣ K J 7 6 2
♠ Q 7                                   ♠ K 9 6 5
♡ 10 9                                  ♡ J 8 7 4
◇ Q 10 9 8 4 2                          ◇ 7 6 5
♣ A 8 3                                 ♣ Q 5
                    ♠ A 8 4 3
                    ♡ K 5 3
                    ◇ A J 3
                    ♣ 10 9 4
```

South	West	North	East
—	—	1 ♣	Pass
2NT	Pass	3NT	Pass
Pass	Pass		

West leads the 10 of diamonds, won by dummy's king.

You have at least six top tricks and three more can be established in clubs. If the club queen is held by West nothing can go wrong, as he cannot embarrass you in diamonds. The danger is that East will capture the first club and lead a diamond through the A J.

In other words, this is one of those hands where if the finesse is working there is no need to take it. Lead a low club from dummy at trick two. If East goes in with the queen, good luck to him, perhaps you should ask him for a game some time.

One attractive possibility is that East will fail to play the queen and West will hold up the ace. Then, of course, knowing that the queen is held by East, you may bring it down on the next round and lose only one trick in the suit. In this case you will probably end up with eleven tricks and East–West will need to do a little explaining to their team-mates at half time.

Question No 7

Dealer East   Love all

                    ♠ K 10 6
                    ♡ Q 9
                    ♢ K J 10 5
                    ♣ K Q 4 2
    ♠ 4 led
                    ♠ J 3
                    ♡ A 7 4
                    ♢ A Q 9 7 2
                    ♣ 8 7 5

The bidding

South	West	North	East
—	—	—	Pass
Pass	Pass	1 ♢	Pass
2NT[1]	Pass	Pass	Pass
Pass	Pass		

Final contract – 3NT

[1] You don't like it? Maybe, but three diamonds is not ideal
either.

The early play

West leads the 4 of spades, you play low from dummy, and East
wins with the queen. He returns the 7 of spades, on which you
play the jack and West the 2.

Preliminary analysis

The play has not started well for your side and you may be wondering how in the post-mortem you will defend your 3NT response. It looks as though West has led from a five-card suit and that as soon as they come in they will make the ace of clubs and three more tricks in spades.

                          ♠ K 10 6
                          ♡ Q 9
                          ◇ K J 10 5
                          ♣ K Q 4 2

   ♠ A 9 8 4 2   ♠ Q 7 5
   ♡ K 6 3 2   ♡ J 10 8 5
   ◇ 6   ◇ 8 4 3
   ♣ J 6 3   ♣ A 10 9

                          ♠ J 3
                          ♡ A 7 4
                          ◇ A Q 9 7 2
                          ♣ 8 7 5

South	West	North	East
—	—	—	Pass
Pass	Pass	1 ◇	Pass
3NT	Pass	Pass	Pass

West leads his fourth best spade, dummy plays low and East wins with the queen. He returns a spade, on which West plays the 2.

You have only seven tricks on top and it is going to be difficult to exert any pressure. If you cash your diamonds West can spare two hearts and two clubs.

The legitimate chances are practically zero, but when the deal came up in a late night rubber game the declarer succeeded. Knowing West to be a studious player, he won the second spade in dummy and returned – a spade!

West, who knew all about suicide squeezes, decided not to embarrass his partner by cashing his two winning spades. (He didn't know, of course, that his partner held the ace of clubs.)

He exited with a club, which went to the king and ace. East returned the club 10 – which was allowed to hold. Now South had nine tricks by way of one spade, one heart, five diamonds and two clubs.

East criticized his partner, but as West pointed out, a heart back after the ace of clubs would also have defeated the contract.

Question No 8

Dealer North   Love all

♠ 8 5 3
♡ K Q 7 4
♢ A Q
♣ A Q J 3

♢ 10 led

♠ A 10 4
♡ A J 9 5
♢ K 3
♣ K 9 8 5

The bidding

South	West	North	East
—	—	1 ♣	Pass
1 ♡	Pass	3 ♡	Pass
6 ♡[1]	Pass	Pass	Pass

Final contract – Six Hearts

[1] Most players would go a-fishing, but since you intend to reach a slam anyway, and since a contract in hearts can hardly be inferior to a contract in clubs, it is sensible to go straight to Six Hearts.

The early play

West leads the 10 of diamonds, won by dummy's ace. Nothing sinister occurs when in time you play hearts or clubs; both suits split 3–2.

Preliminary analysis

Hands where both players have identical shape are usually disappointing in play, and here it seems as though you are likely to lose two tricks in spades. There may be chances for elimination play, and the problem is to play your cards in the best order.

                    ♠ 8 5 3
                    ♡ K Q 7 4
                    ♢ A Q
                    ♣ A Q J 3

♠ K 9   ♠ Q J 7 6 2
♡ 8 6 2   ♡ 10 3
♢ 10 9 8 5 2   ♢ J 7 6 4
♣ 10 7 6   ♣ 4 2

                    ♠ A 10 4
                    ♡ A J 9 5
                    ♢ K 3
                    ♣ K 9 8 5

South	*West*	*North*	*East*
—	—	1 ♣	Pass
1 ♡	Pass	3 ♡	Pass
6 ♡	Pass	Pass	Pass

West leads the 10 of diamonds and you win in dummy.

If the spades are 4–3 you won't have much chance in this contract, but if they are 5–2 there will be various elimination possibilities. Assuming that the trumps break 3–2, you will be able to draw trumps, eliminate the minor suits, and play ace another spade; this will be fatal for a defender who holds a doubleton honour in spades, such as K J or Q J.

However, contracts of this type can often be made when the cards do not lie so favourably. If on the present hand you laboriously draw trumps, then play three rounds of clubs, followed by ace and another spade, it will be easy for West to unblock the king of spades.

The best play, probably, is to win the diamond lead in dummy and immediately play a spade to the ace; quite difficult, now, for West to make an 'advance unblock'.

The resourceful Swiss player, Jean Besse, has noted that it is possible to make 'psychic' plays of this kind. For example, with x x x of a side suit in dummy, A J x in hand, the early play of the ace may induce West, with K x or Q x, to unblock on an occasion when he cannot afford to do so.

3

Concealing strength or weakness

There are several situations in which declarer might wish to conceal his strength in a suit, and a variety of ways in which he can attempt to do so. One reason could be to gain a valuable tempo. Suppose that in a notrump contract a suit is distributed:

A 5

J 9 6 3   10 4

K Q 8 7 2

If West leads the 3 to the 5 and 10, we are effectively in the same position as in an earlier example. The suit is almost certainly dividing 4–2 and as we must lose a trick, now is the time to do so. If we follow smoothly with the 7 it is almost certain that East will continue, placing his partner with queen jack to five. The required tempo is duly gained.

Take the situation where you lead a king and dummy goes down with 10 x x in the suit. If your king scores do you not automatically assume that partner must hold either the ace or the jack? Most defenders certainly would think that and would continue the suit unless they had a really obvious alternative. It follows that declarer, holding A J x, can afford to duck without giving up his second trick. Meanwhile he gains a tempo and also keeps better control of the hand.

On the following deal you are not so much worried about gaining a tempo as about avoiding what you know will be a killing switch.

```
            ♠ 8 5 3 2
            ♡ K 8
            ◇ K 6 3
            ♣ 10 6 5 3
♠ K 6 4                      ♠ A Q 9 7
♡ Q 6 5                      ♡ 7 3 2
◇ Q 8 5 2                    ◇ 10 9 4
♣ A 9 4                      ♣ K Q 8
            ♠ J 10
            ♡ A J 10 9 4
            ◇ A J 7
            ♣ J 7 2
```

Against your 1NT, West leads the 2 of diamonds to East's 9 and your jack. If the hearts come in you will have no problem, but if they do not the defence will doubtless switch to clubs or spades, either of which will beat you. What happens, however, if you win the first diamond with the ace? If West wins the queen of hearts he will probably lead a second round of diamonds. After all, from his point of view this defence is a sure thing, while anything else is at least slightly risky. If he does continue diamonds he not only gives you your seventh trick but also the entry back to hand to cash the hearts.

Often, as in the last example, if you let the defence know the true position they will realize that a desperation switch or cash-out can cost nothing. If on the other hand you conceal your strength they may well be lulled into a false feeling of security and not realize that desperate measures are called for.

Most people would play a suit like A K 4 opposite 8 7 5 3 2 by cashing the ace king and leading a third round to clear the suit. This is all very well, but it does give away rather a lot of information. Assuming that entries permit, you can equally well lead the 4 from hand, giving up the first round instead. Now the defence will probably not place you with both the ace and king and may go astray. Ace followed by 4 is another possibility.

Similarly, when a suit is distributed K 3 opposite A 8 7 5 4 2, try the effect of leading the 3 and ducking it. The defenders' instinctive reaction will be to place you with a small doubleton.

Conceding the trick early is a sound principle to follow, as the earlier the defence comes in the less information they have to work with and the harder it will be for them to find the best play.

```
                    ♠ Q 7 6
                    ♡ 10 9 5
                    ◇ A Q 10 5 2
                    ♣ 6 2
  ♠ 8 3 2                              ♠ J 10 9 4
  ♡ Q 8 6 4 3 2                        ♡ K 7
  ◇ —                                  ◇ J 9 8 7
  ♣ A K 9 3                            ♣ Q 7 5
                    ♠ A K 5
                    ♡ A J
                    ◇ K 6 4 3
                    ♣ J 10 8 4
```

South	West	North	East
1 ◇	1 ♡	2 ◇	Pass
2NT	Pass	3NT	All pass

West leads a low heart to the king and ace. It may look as though it couldn't matter, but if your next play is the king of diamonds you can say goodbye to your contract. When you next duck a diamond, East will win and return a heart. Now West will see that there is no future in clearing the hearts as you must have nine tricks. Instead, he will make the desperation switch to clubs and down you will go. Now see the difference if you lead a

55

low diamond at trick two. When West shows out you play the 10. East again returns a heart, but this time West will probably continue hearts; it will look as though East has the king of diamonds, in which case there is no need to switch.

Matchpoint pairs creates another kind of problem. Even when your contract is assured it will often be worth a lot of points if you can manage to steal an extra trick.

```
                    ♠ K Q 2
                    ♡ 10
                    ◇ A Q J 5 4
                    ♣ J 9 8 7
    ♠ J 10 9                      ♠ 8 7 6 5
    ♡ A K 3 2                     ♡ 6 5 4
    ◇ 6 3 2                       ◇ 9 8 7
    ♣ A 6 5                       ♣ K 4 3
                    ♠ A 4 3
                    ♡ Q J 9 8 7
                    ◇ K 10
                    ♣ Q 10 2
```

South	North
1NT	3NT
Pass	

West leads the jack of spades to dummy's king and wins the first heart to continue spades. Suppose you win and play another heart, pitching one of dummy's clubs as West wins. West will surely view dummy's diamond suit with some foreboding and give up on trying to break 3NT. Instead he will cash out ace and another club, thereby holding you to nine tricks.

The key here is not to be too greedy. Try pitching a diamond on the second heart instead of a club. If West falls for it and

56

assumes that his partner has the king of diamonds he will see no reason not to clear the spades. By throwing away your eleventh trick you greatly improve your chances of making ten tricks, which should be enough for a good score as without your little piece of deception the defence is fairly straightforward.

Concealing strength in one suit and concealing weakness in another are often two sides of the same coin.

<table>
<tr><td>♠ A K Q 5</td><td>♠ J 8 3</td></tr>
<tr><td>♡ K J 10 4</td><td>♡ Q 9 8 7 6 5</td></tr>
<tr><td>♢ A 8</td><td>♢ —</td></tr>
<tr><td>♣ 9 6 3</td><td>♣ 10 7 4 2</td></tr>
</table>

You play in 4♡ and North leads the king of diamonds. Ten tricks are there for the taking, the problem being that you are all too likely to lose four first. Can you do anything about it? Your best chance is to throw a spade from dummy rather than the obvious club. Now when you play a heart to a defender's ace there is a fair chance that he will switch to spades, thinking that is your weak spot. Having drawn the last trump you can now throw two of dummy's clubs on your spades. Bear in mind that a defender will always be tempted to attack a suit where you have discarded.

Concealing a weakness is as often as not a question of looking confident. A king is led against notrumps and you hold A x opposite x x. There is no point in holding up, just win and set about your business. You will be surprised how often the opening leader gets a fixation that you must have something else in the suit – 'no one' parts with an unsupported ace on the first round!

If right-hand opponent leads through your Q x and dummy has nothing, play the queen. Occasionally you will find that right-hand opponent has underled the A K, so the play is technically correct anyway. Just as often the queen will lose and left-hand opponent will switch. Your smooth play of the queen created an illusion of extra strength behind it.

Sometimes only an outrageous bluff can succeed. The ace is led and you hold x x x or 10 x x opposite dummy's Q x – try 'unblocking' the queen. If left-hand opponent does not have the jack he may well be taken in and you have very little to lose.

```
                    ♠ 10 6 2
                    ♡ A K
                    ◇ A 10 8 7 3
                    ♣ K 6 2
    ♠ K J 5 3                        ♠ A 9 8 4
    ♡ 7 6                            ♡ Q 10 5 3
    ◇ J 4 2                          ◇ Q 6
    ♣ Q 10 7 3                       ♣ 9 8 4
                    ♠ Q 7
                    ♡ J 9 8 4 2
                    ◇ K 9 5
                    ♣ A J 5
```

South	North
—	1◇
1♡	2◇
2NT	3NT
Pass	

West leads a low club to the 8 and your jack. Short of a miracle in one of the red suits, you are almost certainly doomed to defeat as whichever defender gets in will switch to a spade now that clubs are known to be no use. There is just a chance that a bluff may throw the defence off the track. Cross to the ace of hearts and, if no honour falls, play a spade to the queen yourself. In actual play West switched to a diamond – with disastrous consequences for the defence. Look at it from his point of view: you bid hearts and appear to have A Q of spades and A J of clubs, so diamonds must be your weak spot. Even if you don't get the magic diamond switch the bluff may still succeed as the defence will be slow to attack spades.

Once again, you had very little to lose as you were almost sure to go down if you played on normal lines. It is extremely entertaining to watch defenders blaming each other after you have brought off this sort of coup.

4

Tempting a misplay

There are many occasions when your chance of success would be greatly improved if you could persuade an opponent to duck the first round of a suit. Frequently this will be the trump suit, as for example in the following deal.

```
♠ K Q J 10 8        ♠ 7 6 5 2
♡ 8 5               ♡ Q J
◇ A K J 10 3        ◇ 7 5 4
♣ 7                 ♣ A 9 6 3
```

West	East
1♠	2♠
4♠	Pass

Keeping the side suit concealed results in a favourable lead, North leading the 2 of diamonds to South's 9 and West's jack. The problem is of course that diamonds appear to be 4–1 and a ruff is imminent. Clearly it would improve things if whoever held the ace of trumps were to duck the first round.

There is no point in trying to fool South. He knows that he had a singleton diamond and will never duck if he holds the ace of spades, so our efforts must be aimed at North, who will not be so certain of the position. If we lead the king of spades North will have no reason to duck, so a lower honour should be chosen. The best card is the queen; from North's point of view this could be from Q J x x x x, in which case he must duck to avoid crashing partner's king.

Superficially it might seem even cleverer to lead the jack or even the 10 as North might not wish to 'waste' his ace on such a low card. The objection to this is that the bidding marks you with higher cards than the 10 and an alert defender will realize that your reason for leading such a low card is that you don't want him to take his ace. It is true that there is some scope here for bluff and double bluff, but fortunately one rarely comes across declarers who think so deeply about the position.

Now, say that South had played the *queen* of diamonds at trick one: should that make any difference to our play? As North cannot be leading from an honour it is almost certain that his 2 is a singleton. There is no longer any point in trying to slip past North's ace of trumps as this time it is he who knows the true position and will surely win the trick and switch to a heart to get his ruff. Instead we should hope that it is South who has A x of trumps. If we cross over to dummy's ace of clubs and lead a trump he may duck in the hope that we have a K J guess – and if we had a slightly different hand he would be right to do so.

The phantom finesse is a common stratagem in notrump contracts as well.

♠ Q 7   ♠ 8 3 2
♡ K Q 5   ♡ A 7 6
♢ Q J 4   ♢ K 10 9 7
♣ A Q 7 6 3   ♣ K J 2

Against your 3NT game, a low heart is led to South's jack. You have eight tricks and the ninth must come from diamonds, the trouble being that a spade switch is very likely and will spell defeat. First, you should win the heart with the king, so leaving both defenders in the dark as to the whereabouts of the queen. They try leading the jack of diamonds – for all the world as

61

though you were about to take a finesse against the queen. This is one of the most common of all deceptive plays and has a very high rate of success. If North does duck his ace you run for home of course as you now have your nine tricks. The 4 of diamonds is a good card too; North may think you have Q x x and intend to finesse the 9.

♠ 10 9   ♠ A 3
♡ A 7   ♡ K 9 6 4 2
◇ K Q J 5 3 ◇ A 7 4
♣ K 10 9 6 ♣ J 8 5

Once again you are in 3NT, and North finds the killing lead of a low spade. Ducking cannot be right as South will win and return a second spade, discovering the exact spade position in the process. The only real chance is to go up with the ace of spades and lead the jack of clubs. At this stage South may not be sure of the actual position and may duck the ace of clubs to give you a guess. In fact you do not have a guess as you need a quick trick without losing the lead, so will put up the king. True, you run the risk of going an extra one down, but that is a small price to pay for giving yourself a chance of making the contract. The chance of success of this play is perhaps not that great, and you might well decide not to risk it at pairs, where the extra undertrick could turn a near average score into a bottom.

Very important, too, is the manner in which you make your play. If you sit for a couple of minutes, sigh, and then play, not only have you given the defence time to think but you have also clearly told them that you have a problem. Play smoothly and confidently as though you don't have a care in the world, and you will be surprised how often you escape from a seemingly hopeless situation. (Mind you, it is possible to go too far in that direction; some declarers play quickly *only* when they aim to deceive.)

The following is a much more subtle example of the phantom finesse.

♠ K 8 7 3   ♠ A 9 6 4
♡ A Q 5   ♡ K J 10 4
◇ A 7 6   ◇ 8 3 2
♣ 7 4 2   ♣ A 9

The queen of diamonds is led against 4♠. You duck, but win the second round and cash the top two spades, to which all follow. Now you will be all right so long as the player with the long trump also has at least three hearts, as you will be able to get rid of your third diamond. Is there any extra chance? Yes, providing that it is South who has the remaining trump. Play the ace of hearts, a heart to the king, and the jack of hearts as though intending to take a ruffing finesse. If South has only two hearts he may discard, seeing no point in trumping a loser. Having slipped the third heart through, you cross to the ace of clubs and take a discard on the fourth one – to gnashings of teeth from all sides.

This is a classic example of putting yourself in a defender's shoes and trying to visualize the hand from his viewpoint. Once you have thought about the defender's problem you are in a position to conjure up a losing option for him.

Try your hand at this one:

♠ K J 5   ♠ 7 2
♡ K 10 5   ♡ Q 7 6
◇ A K 4   ◇ 9 5 3
♣ A K 9 7   ♣ Q J 10 8 5

Against 3NT, North leads the 6 of spades to the queen and your king. You have eight top tricks and can set up a ninth easily enough in hearts, the only danger being that South may win the ace and pump a spade through. Is there any way to divert South if he does hold the ace? Remember that he cannot be sure that the spades are running, so if you give him a reason to duck his ace of hearts he may do so. Cash the A K of clubs and lay down the heart king. With a bit of luck you will look for all the world like a man with no more clubs who is trying to force an entry to the dummy. It won't work if North shows out on clubs of course, but if he has to follow twice even length signals may not solve the defence's difficulties.

Sometimes the declarer's problem will be to avoid a possible block in dummy's long suit. For example:

♠ A K J 7	♠ 5 4 2
♡ A J 5	♡ 10 6 3
◇ 10 9	◇ A K J 6 4
♣ K 5 4 2	♣ 8 3

In 3NT North leads a low club to the queen and king. The spade suit could come to the rescue, but your main chance is to bring in the diamonds. If North has Q x x there will be no problem, but if he has Q x or Q x x x a first-round cover will create an awkward blockage. Rather than lead the 10, which tends to invite a cover, try the 9. North should still cover, but players often fail to cover a card when they think that partner can beat it anyway. If the 9 slips through, a second-round finesse will bring in the entire suit.

Similar play is correct with other combinations.

| J 10 | A Q 6 5 2 |
| Q J | A 10 9 8 5 3 (2) |

In either case, leading the lower honour first may catch

64

North napping. In the second example North, with K x, could block the run of the suit by covering. The general principle is that if you want a defender to duck you play the lower of your touching cards; conversely, if you want him to cover lead the top card.

Q J 9   A 5 2

Wanting three tricks, the only legitimate hope is that either North has a doubleton king or South a doubleton 10, in which case a successful guess will do the job. If you lead the queen, however, you have the significant extra chance that an inexpert North may cover with K x x or K x x x, enabling you to finesse the 9 on the way back. It is true that in general he shouldn't, but as I have said already, if you give them a chance most defenders will fall from grace at least some of the time, and if it costs you nothing why not give them that chance? The essential point is that when you have touching cards one card is almost always better than the other.

In each of these problems the declarer has played in a deceptive manner, and it is up to the defenders to unravel the plot.

Question No 9

Dealer South   Love all

```
                    ♠ A J 9 7 4
                    ♡ A 7 3 2
                    ◇ 4
                    ♣ J 8 2
     ♠ 2
     ♡ K Q 10 4        N
     ◇ A J 10 2    W       E
     ♣ A Q 7 3        S
```

The bidding

South	West	North	East
1♠	dble	4♠	Pass
Pass	Pass		

Final contract – Four Spades

The early play

West leads the king of hearts, dummy wins with the ace, East plays the 6 and South the jack. Declarer leads a diamond to the 8 and 10. How do you defend?

Preliminary analysis

The play to the first trick is at any rate consistent with partner holding four hearts and South a singleton jack. The diamond situation is not altogether clear. Where will four tricks come from?

Answer No 9

```
                    ♠ A J 9 7 4
                    ♡ A 7 3 2
                    ◇ 4
                    ♣ J 8 2
♠ 2                                    ♠ 5 3
♡ K Q 10 4                             ♡ 9 8 6 5
◇ A J 10 2                             ◇ 9 7 6 3
♣ A Q 7 3                              ♣ K 9 5
                    ♠ K Q 10 8 6
                    ♡ J
                    ◇ K Q 8 5
                    ♣ 10 6 4
```

South	West	North	East
1♠	dble	4♠	Pass
Pass	Pass		

Declarer won your heart lead in dummy and led a diamond to his 8 and your 10.

Looking at all four hands, it is easy to see that you must switch to a club, as otherwise declarer will eventually take a ruffing finesse in diamonds to dispose of one of dummy's clubs. Had the declarer played a diamond to the king or queen, this danger would have been more obvious.

Leading a club would cost a trick if South held such as ◇ K Q and ♣ K, but it would only be an overtrick.

When you have made up your mind to lead a club, which card do you think is best? The ace might be a mistake if East held K x and failed to unblock. A low club might cause some partners to insert the 9 from K 9 x. A small point, but perhaps the queen is the safest card.

Question No 10

Dealer South   Game all

♠ 7 6 2
♡ A K 3
◇ K 8 5 4
♣ Q J 6

♠ J 10 9 8 4
♡ 9 8 2
◇ A 7 3
♣ 7 4

```
      N
  W       E
      S
```

The bidding

South	West	North	East
1NT[1]	Pass	3NT	Pass
Pass	Pass		

Final contract – 3NT

[1] Weak, 12–14.

The early play

West's lead of the jack of spades runs to the king and ace. At trick two South advances the 10 of diamonds.

Preliminary analysis

A nasty card, this 10 of diamonds! Are you ready to duck without giving any indication, or will you take the ace and, if so, what will you do next?

```
                    ♠ 7 6 2
                    ♡ A K 3
                    ◇ K 8 5 4
                    ♣ Q J 6
♠ J 10 9 8 4                        ♠ K 5 3
♡ 9 8 2                            ♡ J 6 5 4
◇ A 7 3                            ◇ 9 6
♣ 7 4                             ♣ A 9 8 3
                    ♠ A Q
                    ♡ Q 10 7
                    ◇ Q J 10 2
                    ♣ K 10 5 2
```

West's lead of the jack of spades is covered by the king and ace. South then leads the 10 of diamonds.

If South can slip through the 10 of diamonds he will immediately switch to clubs and develop nine tricks before the defenders can do him any damage. The 10 of diamonds is a slightly better card than the jack, because it leaves open the possibility that declarer has Q 10 9 as an alternative to J 10.

Most players would instinctively play low with the West hand, but there is a good reason why he should win and lead a second spade. You don't see it? Well, it should have registered on you at once that declarer probably has ♠ A Q alone, because with A Q x he would have held up for one round.

You may say that perhaps the declarer has J 10 x in diamonds and is simply looking for an extra trick in that suit. The answer to this is that declarer would surely leave till later the play of a suit in which he had to take a view. To play the ace of diamonds on the 10 would be a mistake only if South held something like J 10 9 x x in diamonds and East a singleton queen.

Question No 11

Dealer South   Love all

```
            ♠ K Q 5
            ♡ K Q 8 7 2
            ◇ K 2
            ♣ A Q 4
                            ♠ 9 7 6
♣ 5 led       ┌─────────┐   ♡ 4
              │    N    │   ◇ J 10 8 6 4
              │ W     E │   ♣ J 10 7 3
              │    S    │
              └─────────┘
```

The bidding

South	West	North	East
1NT¹	Pass	3♡	Pass
4◇²	Pass	4NT³	Pass
5♠	Pass	5NT	Pass
6◇	Pass	7NT	Pass
Pass	Pass		

Final contract – 7NT

¹ 16–18.
² Support for hearts, control in diamonds.
³ Conventional, when following a force.

The early play

The lead of the 5 of clubs is won by the queen, South dropping the 8. Declarer plays ace and king of hearts, on which you throw a diamond, then queen of hearts, on which you throw a spade. Three top spades now follow. What do you discard on the third round?

Preliminary analysis

It looks as though South began with A x x in both major suits. He might hold A Q x in diamonds and K x x x in clubs, or A Q x x and K x x. The question is, which?

♠ K Q 5
♥ K Q 8 7 2
♦ K 2
♣ A Q 4

♠ J 8 4 2   ♠ 9 7 6
♥ J 10 6 5   ♥ 4
♦ 9 3   ♦ J 10 8 6 4
♣ 6 5 2   ♣ J 10 7 3

♠ A 10 3
♥ A 9 3
♦ A Q 7 5
♣ K 9 8

South	West	North	East
1NT	Pass	3♥	Pass
4♦	Pass	4NT	Pass
5♣	Pass	5NT	Pass
6♦	Pass	7NT	Pass
Pass	Pass		

West's lead of the 5 of clubs is won by dummy's queen. South plays ace, king and queen of hearts, East discarding a diamond and a spade, then three rounds of spades.

The declarer has played his cards in the best order, forcing you to make a critical discard before you know whether you can spare another diamond or a club. Does South hold four diamonds and three clubs, or the other way round?

At the table East discarded another diamond, arguing that his partner's 5 of clubs suggested a doubleton 5 2. However, players who are leading against a grand slam don't always produce the orthodox card. There was a better indication: West is marked with eight cards in the major suits; defending against a grand slam he would surely lead from three small rather than from a doubleton that might kill partner's J x x x or J 10 x x or even Q 10 x x. East should play his partner for three clubs, therefore, and discard a club, not a diamond.

Question No 12

Dealer South   Love all

        ♠ J 9 3
        ♡ K 9 4
        ◇ A 9 8 3
        ♣ K 6 2

♠ Q 8 6 2
♡ 5
◇ Q 7 2
♣ Q J 10 7 5

```
        N
    W       E
        S
```

The bidding

South	West	North	East
2♡[1]	Pass	3♡[2]	Pass
4♡	Pass	6♡	Pass
Pass	Pass		

Final contract – Six Hearts

[1] Acol-type, forcing for one round.
[2] Forcing, includes an ace.

The early play

Your lead of the queen of clubs holds the first trick, partner playing the 3 and declarer the 8. What now?

Preliminary analysis

As the play to the first trick has gone, partner might hold A x x of clubs or even A x. Is that likely, or are you going to play for some other possibility?

77

Answer No 12

       ♠ J 9 3
       ♡ K 9 4
       ◇ A 9 8 3
       ♣ K 6 2

♠ Q 8 6 2   ♠ A 10 7 5 4
♡ 5   ♡ 8 2
◇ Q 7 2   ◇ J 10 5
♣ Q J 10 7 5   ♣ 9 4 3

       ♠ K
       ♡ A Q J 10 7 6 3
       ◇ K 6 4
       ♣ A 8

South	West	North	East
2♡	Pass	3♡	Pass
4♡	Pass	6♡	Pass
Pass	Pass		

West leads the queen of clubs, East playing the 3 and declarer the 8.

It is tempting for West to play a second club, but there are dangers in this, as the diagram shows. South will win with the ace of clubs, later discard a diamond on the king of clubs, and establish a long diamond, on which the king of spades will disappear.

If you led a second club you would be playing South for something like:

       ♠ A K
       ♡ A Q J 10 x x x
       ◇ K x
       ♣ x x

78

With a hand of that sort, containing two club losers, would he go straight to six hearts over four hearts? Some might, but the majority would start a cue-bidding sequence with 3♠, intending to follow with 4♢ over 4♣. You cannot be sure what is happening, it is true, unless partner looks surprised when your queen holds the first trick. If this happens, you must just clench your teeth and play a second round of clubs. Otherwise, your reputation will be mud.

Question No 13

Dealer South   Love all

```
                    ♠ Q 8 2
                    ♡ 7 4
                    ◇ K 9 6 5 4 2
                    ♣ 7 4
♠ J 7 5 4         ┌─────────────┐
♡ A K Q 10        │      N      │
◇ Q 7             │  W       E  │
♣ J 8 2           │      S      │
                  └─────────────┘
```

The bidding

South	West	North	East
1♣	Pass	1◇	Pass
2NT	Pass	3◇[1]	Pass
3NT	Pass	Pass	Pass

Final contract – 3NT

[1] This is a weak bid in the Acol system, but partners sometimes persist.

The early play

Sitting West, you begin with two top hearts, on which partner plays 6 and 2, declarer 5 and J. When you cash a third heart both players follow.

Preliminary analysis

It is clear that East began with four small hearts and South with J x x. Can you think of any reason why South should have dropped the jack on the second round? What do you play next?

Answer No 13

```
                    ♠ Q 8 2
                    ♡ 7 4
                    ◇ K 9 6 5 4 2
                    ♣ 7 4
♠ J 7 5 4                           ♠ K 9 6
♡ A K Q 10                          ♡ 9 6 3 2
◇ Q 7                               ◇ 8 3
♣ J 8 2                             ♣ Q 10 5 3
                    ♠ A 10 3
                    ♡ J 8 5
                    ◇ A J 10
                    ♣ A K 9 6
```

South	West	North	East
1♣	Pass	1◇	Pass
2NT	Pass	3◇	Pass
3NT	Pass	Pass	Pass

West begins with two top hearts, East playing high-low, South the 5 and jack. On the third round dummy discards a club and the others follow suit.

Why did declarer drop the jack on the second round of hearts? He wanted to make it easier for you to continue the suit, relieving you of any worry that he might hold J x x x. He wanted you to cash the fourth round so that he could discard the embarrassing 10 of diamonds, which threatened to block the run of the suit. You lay the fourth heart on one side, therefore, and exit with a low club. If South tries to slip through a sneaky 10 of diamonds you cover with the queen.

South's play of the jack of hearts on the second round was not particularly clever: it should have warned you that he had a problem of some kind.

Question No 14

Dealer South   Love all

```
              ♠ K 10 9 3
              ♡ 8 6 2
              ◇ A J 10
              ♣ A Q 3
♠ 7
♡ A J 9              ┌─────────┐
◇ 8 6 4             │    N    │
♣ J 10 9 7 5 2      │ W     E │
                    │    S    │
                    └─────────┘
```

The bidding

South	West	North	East
1♠	Pass	4♣[1]	Pass
4◇[2]	Pass	4♠	Pass
4NT	Pass	5♡	Pass
6♠	Pass	Pass	Pass

Final contract – Six Spades

[1] Swiss convention, showing a raise to four spades with slam possibilities.
[2] Confirming slam prospects.

The early play

Declarer wins the club lead, ruffs a club, and draws two rounds of trumps. He plays ◇ 10 to the king, ◇ 9 to the jack, ruffs the third club, and plays ◇ Q to the ace, partner following with the 2, 3, 5. Then a low heart goes to the 4 and king.

Preliminary analysis

You have been following suit, but now you have to make a decision: will you take the ace of hearts or will you duck?

Answer No 14

$\spadesuit$ K 10 9 3
$\heartsuit$ 8 6 2
$\diamondsuit$ A J 10
$\clubsuit$ A Q 3

$\spadesuit$ 7
$\heartsuit$ A J 9
$\diamondsuit$ 8 6 4
$\clubsuit$ J 10 9 7 5 2

$\spadesuit$ 8 5
$\heartsuit$ Q 10 7 5 4
$\diamondsuit$ 5 3 2
$\clubsuit$ K 8 6

$\spadesuit$ A Q J 6 4 2
$\heartsuit$ K 3
$\diamondsuit$ K Q 9 7
$\clubsuit$ 4

South	West	North	East
1$\spadesuit$	Pass	4$\clubsuit$	Pass
4$\diamondsuit$	Pass	4$\spadesuit$	Pass
4NT	Pass	5$\heartsuit$	Pass
6$\spadesuit$	Pass	Pass	Pass

South wins the club lead, ruffs a club, and draws trumps. He leads the 10 of diamonds to the king, the 9 to the jack, ruffs the third club and plays $\diamondsuit$ Q to the ace. East has followed with the 2, 3 and 5. Then a low heart goes to the 4 and king.

Sitting West, you have a tricky decision. If South has only three diamonds his shape will be 6–3–3–1 and you will need to hold off the king of hearts because he might hold K Q 10.

South has played the hand in a slightly confusing way and the only indication you have is that East has played 2, 3, 5 of diamonds in that order. This should mean that East has 2–5–3–3 distribution and you can play South for a doubleton heart, not K Q 10. If this turns out to be wrong, you will at least have the melancholy satisfaction of being able to blame partner.

Dealer South   Game all

    ♠ K 10 9 4
    ♡ J 6 3
    ♢ J 7 5 2
    ♣ A 7

                     ♠ 8 3
♡ 10 led   N   ♡ Q 5 4 2
      W   E   ♢ K 10 3
        S   ♣ Q 9 8 5

The bidding

South	West	North	East
2NT	Pass	3♣	Pass
3♢	Pass	3♠	Pass
3NT	Pass	4♢	Pass
6♢	Pass	Pass	Pass

Final contract – Six Diamonds

The early play

West's lead of the 10 of hearts is covered by the J, Q and A. Declarer plays a club to the ace, a diamond to the queen, and cashes the ace of diamonds, partner following. Then he plays ace of spades, a spade to the king, and the 10 of spades from dummy.

Preliminary analysis

It looks as though South (who has denied a 4-card major) began with A Q 9 x of diamonds and K 10 x x or K J x x of clubs. If the rest of his hand is ♠ A J and ♡ A K x, you must discard on this lead of the third spade; but if it is ♠ A Q J and ♡ A x you must ruff promptly and cash the heart trick. Which is more likely?

♠ K 10 9 4
♥ J 6 3
♦ J 7 5 2
♣ A 7

♠ 7 6 5 2   ♠ 8 3
♥ K 10 9 7   ♥ Q 5 4 2
♦ 8 6   ♦ K 10 3
♣ 10 6 4   ♣ Q 9 8 5

♠ A Q J
♥ A 8
♦ A Q 9 4
♣ K J 3 2

South	West	North	East
2NT	Pass	3♣	Pass
3♦	Pass	3♠	Pass
3NT	Pass	4♦	Pass
6♦	Pass	Pass	Pass

West's lead of the 10 of hearts is covered by the jack, queen and ace. Declarer crosses to the ace of clubs, finesses the queen of diamonds and cashes the ace. Then he plays ace of spades, jack to the king, and the 10 of spades from dummy.

If, as East, you let this pass, South will make his contract, as his heart loser will go away on the fourth spade. On the other hand, if you ruff and South's holding in the majors is ♠ A J and ♥ A K x, then it will be fatal to ruff prematurely with master trump.

You may say, 'If my partner has shown four spades by playing high-low, I shall know what to do.' That is true and it confirms the point that has been made before – that the defender with the weak hand should normally play 'true' cards to help his partner.

But suppose you cannot rely on your partner to have signalled in this way. The best clue then is that South, with ♠ A J and ♡ A K x, would probably not have played the jack of hearts from dummy at trick one. At any rate, he would have considered the matter very carefully. On all grounds, it is probably right for East to nip in with the king of diamonds.

Dealer South   E–W vulnerable

♠ K Q 10 7 4 2
♥ 6
♦ A 7 4 3
♣ 5 2

♠ 9 8 3
♥ 8 7 2
♦ K Q J 9
♣ A 9 7

```
        N
    W       E
        S
```

The bidding

South	West	North	East
1♥	Pass	1♠	Pass
4♥	Pass	Pass	Pass

Final contract – Four Hearts

The early play

You lead the king of diamonds, which is followed by the 3, 5, 6. What next?

Preliminary analysis

If this were not a problem I dare say you would follow sharply with the queen (or jack) of diamonds, to remove dummy's entry. This might be right, but are you sure?

♠ K Q 10 7 4 2
♡ 6
♢ A 7 4 3
♣ 5 2

♠ 9 8 3   ♠ J 6 5
♡ 8 7 2   ♡ A 10
♢ K Q J 9   ♢ 10 8 5 2
♣ A 9 7   ♣ J 10 8 4

♠ A
♡ K Q J 9 5 4 3
♢ 6
♣ K Q 6 3

South	West	North	East
1♡	Pass	1♠	Pass
4♡	Pass	Pass	Pass

South might have opened two hearts, but perhaps he is playing weak two bids, or perhaps he doesn't like to open a strong two bid with only one ace.

The king of diamonds holds the first trick, East playing the 5 and declarer the 6.

You can see what will happen if you continue joyfully with a second diamond: declarer will discard the ace of spades on the ace of diamonds, discard two clubs on high spades, and lose just three tricks

It would be right to continue diamonds if South held such as:

♠ A
♡ A K J 10 x x x
♢ x x x
♣ K J

With this hand there would be no point in holding off the first diamond, risking a diamond continuation and a ruff.

Suppose you decide to switch, what will you lead at trick two? Your side will have to play a trump eventually (to stop club ruffs), so a trump now is as good as anything.

5

Gaining – or saving – a trick

Sometimes a key suit is distributed in such a way that declarer is destined to lose a certain number of tricks however he handles it, assuming accurate defence. If he cannot afford that number of losers he must hope to find a lie of the cards where he can induce a defensive error to save a trick. One possibility is that the defenders may be persuaded to crash their honours, as in this example:

A 10 9 8 5 4 2   J 6 3

If declarer leads a low card from the dummy he will always lose at least one trick as South will never play an honour unless forced to do so. If however you lead the jack he may be tempted into covering with Q x or K x, particularly if the bidding has not disclosed your great length in the suit. After all, you might have played the same way with A Q 9 8 x in which case the cover would be essential to promote North's 10. The example may appear trivial, yet I wonder how many people would always try it. You might as well as it costs nothing, and even if it works only one time in a hundred that's still all profit.

To play a suit of J 9 7 5 4 2 opposite Q 6 3 for only one loser may seem impossible, yet the situation is similar to the previous example and there is a chance. Playing to hold yourself to two losers you would start by leading a low card through the defender you thought more likely to be short in the suit. Obviously that is no good when you can only afford one loser – something more dramatic is required. Try leading the queen off the dummy. Will not the next hand be at least tempted to cover with K 10 8? With your actual holding, if he does so he will crash his partner's bare ace and you will be able to finesse the 9 on the second round. The point is that you might have started with A J 9 x x x, where the cover is necessary to leave you with a second-round guess.

In general, in these sort of situations where you are trying to bring in a suit in which you are missing K 10 to four or five, it is technically correct to lead a low card for the first finesse. The difference in the odds is often fairly small however and leading the honour can be the right practical play even though it is anti-percentage. The point is that sometimes a defender will be afraid of crashing his partner's honour and so may fail to cover when in a double-dummy situation he should do so. For example, if you actually did have A Q 9 8 2 opposite J 7 3, South might fail to cover the jack with K 10 x, thereby saving you any later guess. If you play different card combinations in identical fashions you may not be going with the theoretical odds but you will certainly give the defence some awkward decisions.

Actually you are not just giving the defender a guess, as if he thinks it through he may well come up with the right answer most of the time – you are also playing on his instincts in two ways. First, many players are not prepared to stop and think through every defensive problem. They believe, and quite rightly, that to stop and think will often solve declarer's guess for him, so they prefer to play quickly as though they did not have a problem themselves. You are therefore playing on their fear of giving away information. Second, even experienced players occasionally fall prey to the reflex action of covering an honour with an honour; it is something that is drummed into all of us when we take up the game and for some it is a tough habit to break.

You can use the same principle to give yourself a slight extra chance with a suit like this:

A K Q 7 4 2   10 6 3

What can it cost to lead the 10 first? *You* know that you do not intend to run it, but an unwary defender could be caught napping with J 9 8 5. He clearly shouldn't, as this time he cannot hope to achieve anything, but that reflex is a powerful thing.

With A K 7 5 2 opposite 9 6 4, running the 9 is actually the best technical play as it saves a trick when North has the bare 8. It saves a trick even more often because players have been known to cover with Q 10 8 3, J 10 8 3, or even Q J 8 3.

It is surprising how often the right technical play is also the correct psychological play. Let us suppose that South originally opened 1NT so that we know he must have at least two cards in the key suit. What is the right play with A 9 8 7 3 opposite J 6 4 2? The technical answer is to run the jack as this gains a trick when North has the singleton 10. If North has the singleton king or queen declarer appears doomed to lose two tricks however he tackles the suit, but wait – that leaves South with Q 10 5 or K 10 5. Will he not be tempted to cover the jack at least some of the time?

If we change things around slightly we find a new possibility:

A 9 8 7 6 4   J 3

Technically, running the jack is still correct as it saves a trick when North has the bare 10, but it no longer has quite the same crashing potential as few defenders will cover with Q 10 5 2 or K 10 5 2. Still, if South is known to have the length it is worth trying. Suppose however that it was North who opened 1NT and is therefore marked with some length in the suit. Now running the jack will achieve nothing. If you need to play the suit for one loser the correct play is low towards the jack. First, from a technical viewpoint, North is powerless if he holds Q 10 or K 10 doubleton – try it and see. Second, it is the best chance of inducing a defensive mistake. Suppose that North holds

95

Q x x, might he not rise with the queen? He would be right to do so if you held A K.

The bidding, and in some cases the opening lead, may give a useful indication which opponent is more likely to have length in the suit you are interested in. As we have already seen, this can affect which opponent you should aim to trap.

10 9 8 5 2   J 7 6

If South appears to hold the length you should start with the jack from the dummy. Who knows, he might rise from K Q 4 3 or A Q 4 3 and crash his partner's honour; he is most unlikely to do this if you lead a low card. If however it is North who has the length, leading the jack will achieve nothing. Now the best play is to cross to hand and lead low towards the jack. If North has K Q 4 3 or similar he will know that he does not have to go in with an honour on the first round, but he may do so anyway, perhaps because he does not wish to risk losing a tempo in the play, perhaps just because he is asleep. The reason is immaterial – if he does play a high card he will save you a trick. This is the basic principle when trying to crash opponents' honour cards: lead the first round *through* the defender you think has the greater length. Sometimes that will succeed, the reverse cannot.

Sometimes a defender's bidding will render him open to deception. Perhaps you opened one spade. North overcalled 1NT, and you eventually become declarer in a spade contract with one of these two spade holdings:

(1) Q J 10 8 5 4   9 7 6 3

(2) A Q J 10 8 4   9 7 6 3

Since you know that North has a spade stopper you can play

terrible games with his nerves by leading the queen with both these holdings. Imagine his torment holding K x. He knows you are doing something, but what? In the first situation he may even occasionally go in with A x as well if he is afraid that to be left with a bare ace may leave him open to an endplay.

There is one situation where it is sometimes possible to persuade the defence to crash their trump honours without actually leading the suit. The principle comes up repeatedly in bridge literature, so one example should suffice.

```
                    ♠ Q J 7 4
                    ♡ A 6
                    ♢ K Q 8 6 2
                    ♣ K J
    ♠ A 5 3                         ♠ K
    ♡ Q 9 7 3 2                     ♡ J 10 8 4
    ♢ J 9 7 3                       ♢ 10 4
    ♣ 6                             ♣ A 10 9 7 5 3
                    ♠ 10 9 8 6 2
                    ♡ K 5
                    ♢ A 5
                    ♣ Q 8 4 2
```

Against South's four spades, West leads his singleton club and ruffs the return. He switches to a low heart. How should South play?

Simply to play on trumps is unlikely to succeed, but there is an excellent chance if West is down to a doubleton honour. Win with dummy's ace of hearts, cross to the ace of diamonds, and lead the queen of clubs. If West thinks you are trying to throw dummy's losing heart he will probably ruff low, enabling you to overruff and lead a trump. Now, if the position was as in the diagram, the ace and king will fall together – and East-West will not be amused.

Suppose declarer has to play a trump suit of 10 7 5 4 2

opposite K 6 3 for two losers. No doubt he will start by playing a low card to the king. If that loses to the ace he may well just shrug his shoulders and give up on the hand, leading the next round from whichever hand he happens to be in. In fact, by leading the second round from the dummy there is still a chance of restricting the trump losers to two. If South began with A Q x, particularly A Q 9 where he knows declarer has no real guess, he may lazily go in with the queen, crashing his partner's jack. On occasions he may have a perfectly plausible reason for such a play, as he may be afraid that ducking would give declarer a valuable tempo. The thing to remember is that the defenders do not necessarily know as much about the hand as you do and may think that the point of the hand is totally different from the actual one.

Up to now, examples in this section have revolved around the handling of the trump suit, though most would be equally valid in notrump. There is also a number of ploys one can try to gain a trick in a side suit. The 'crashing' plays already discussed are generally applicable to side suits also. Here is one which can succeed only when another suit is trumps:

K J 7 6 3   8 2

Suppose you lead low from dummy and guess to put in the king, which scores. If you have the entries it is worth crossing back to dummy to lead the second round. If South has such as A 10 x x he is under tremendous pressure to play his ace as from his point of view you may hold K Q and if he doesn't take the ace now he is likely to lose it. If he does crash his partner's queen you will have set up the suit one round earlier than you would otherwise have done.

There are other holdings where a defender can be pressured into taking an ace unnecessarily. You hold K 3 opposite Q 7 6 4 and when you lead low to the king it wins. The simple line is to lead the 3 back and duck it, hoping to bring the ace down in two or three rounds. But why not cross to dummy and lead low from the queen on the second round? South may go in with the ace for fear that your actual holding is K J doubleton, especially as his partner will often have given him a count on the suit. If you have the entries this is a cost-nothing play.

The same principle can be exploited in the next example. Say you have a small singleton opposite dummy's K Q x x x and from the bidding you are sure that the ace is offside. If you can afford it why not try leading low from the K Q? If South has the ace but not the jack he may play it to guard against your having a singleton jack.

The majority of players, needing two tricks from 7 3 opposite A Q 6 4, would finesse the queen. If they could afford a loser, a few would cash the ace first, then lead towards the queen. An alternative which is technically just as good as the latter play is to lead low away from the A Q on the first round. South will be afraid of losing his king and may sometimes rise with it, particularly if it is doubleton. If nothing exciting happens you can still fall back on a second-round finesse, so the play has cost nothing. The ploy is equally valid in a side suit or in notrump, and even when it doesn't actually work you may learn something useful from how smoothly South plays to the trick. If he has the king he will rarely be able to play low without at least some thought.

The principle of playing the card you are known to hold was covered in an earlier chapter, but it crops up again here in a slightly different guise. For example, you hold Q 10 opposite A 9 6 3 and North leads the jack. The card you are known to hold, from South's point of view, is the queen (assuming that North would lead the queen from Q J). However, jack from J 10 x is quite a normal lead, so if you want to avoid a loser in the suit try rising with the ace and dropping the queen from hand. When you next lead low from the table South is in something of a quandary and may play low, allowing your 10 to win. His problem is that if he plays the king and finds his partner with J 10 x a further ruff will set up dummy's 9 as a trick.

There are many situations where the same principle can be applied, the most familiar being:

J 10   A Q 5 2

If the king is marked in the South hand the only hope is to lead the jack and put the ace on it (or to lead the ace from dummy). When you lead low to the 10 South may not play his king, especially if North has not conscientiously indicated his length.

We have seen that leading an honour can sometimes induce an unwise cover by a defender. The reverse side of the coin is that if a defender thinks that you are about to take a losing finesse he may fail to cover when he should have done. We saw this earlier when we were trying to steal a trick without losing the lead. Here is a slightly different situation:

The normal play with K Q 9 6 3 opposite J 2 is to lead low towards the jack, then low back to the king. This produces four tricks whenever the suit breaks 3–3 or the 10 is doubleton. A better play is to cross to dummy and lead the jack. This still works whenever the normal play does, but it also works if an unwary South fails to rise with A x, as the ace is wasted on fresh air on your next lead. This is a fairly common type of defensive error and is well worth playing for.

A more common holding is Q 6 3 opposite J 7 2 or similar. One would like to see the defence open up the suit, but what is the best play if they refuse to do so? The standard play is to lead low to one honour, then low back to the other, succeeding whenever the A K are in the same hand. Often you will have good reason to suspect that the honours are split, perhaps because of the bidding, perhaps because North might have led the suit with A K. In that case the normal play has no chance but a bluff may succeed. Try leading the jack from dummy, as early in the play as possible, before the defenders know much about the hand. If South has both honours you will still succeed, but you will also get a trick when he plays low with A x x (x) hoping that you have a guess in the suit.

Another situation in which leading an unsupported honour may gain a trick is when the defenders think you have entry problems. They will then hesitate to take their high cards until compelled to do so. Suppose you open 2NT and dummy is, as usual, a sorry disappointment – J 10 x x x and out, or something of that nature.

    (1) K 3   J 10 7 6 4

    (2) A Q   J 10 7 6 4

What do you suppose will happen if you confidently lead (1) the king, (2) the queen, from hand. The defence can see that dummy has no outside entry and will amost certainly let you hold the trick to make sure that you can never make use of the long suit. It is important to make your play as early as possible. I may be repeating myself, but I cannot stress enough that the sooner you try to deceive the better is your chance of success. At trick two the defence is in the dark, at trick eight the hand will be an open book or nearly so. Obviously, having stolen your trick, you now look elsewhere for the remainder.

Leading any unsupported honour in a suit where dummy has length has a fair chance of success. Even J 3 opposite 10 9 7 6 2 may be worth a trick if both defenders misjudge the position. For example, North may play low with A Q x, South with K x x.

There are many more positions of the kind described in this chapter. Indeed, with almost all combinations one method of playing may be slightly better than another. If you can work these out for yourself you will never forget them.

6

The art of guessing

Guessing is a very unsatisfactory business. An expert is very rarely faced with a complete guess as there is usually some vague inference to follow, but when he is, even the most gifted player will get it right only half the time. The trick is to persuade the opposition to save you from having to guess wherever possible. Take this hand:

```
♠ A J 10 9 6 4      ♠ K 3
♡ A 7               ♡ 9 8 6 4 3 2
◇ A K 5             ◇ 7 6 3
♣ A 4               ♣ 7 5
```

When North leads the king of clubs against your contract of 4♠, it is clear that your success or failure will be entirely dependent on how you tackle the trump suit. The percentage play is to lead low to the king and finesse on the way back, but you may be able to do better than that. Try the effect of winning with the ace and returning a club at trick two. If the defender who wins the club thinks you are looking to ruff clubs in the dummy he will be eager to switch to trumps. Against weak defenders this is almost a sure thing and obviously saves you a guess. If the defence fails to switch to a trump it could well be because the defender on lead has the queen himself and does not wish to lead away from it. With nothing else to go on, it would therefore be reasonable to play for the player who won the second club to have the trump queen if he did not switch to trumps. This play is less likely to succeed against

102

good players, but is none the less worth considering.

It is possible, in moderate company, to play skilfully with a trump holding such as A J 10 9 2 opposite K 8 4 3. Lead the jack from hand. Only a beginner would cover, of course, but thousands would play in a slightly different fashion with Q x than with x or x x. Most, with no thought of being unfair, would play low very smoothly from Q x or Q x x, deliberately from x x or x x x.

In a like vein, suppose you hold A 10 9 6 opposite K 8 7 3, and when you lead the 10 North produces the jack, what next? Obviously if he has Q J x you cannot win, so your decision is whether to play him for Q J or the bare jack. That is, if he is a competent player. The supporters of the theory of restricted choice will no doubt tell you that you should finesse on the second round as half the time that North began with Q J he would have played the queen, making the bare jack more likely. Against a weak North you have even more reason to finesse as he may have covered with J x, thereby giving you the whole suit for nothing.

The defenders are more likely to save you the trouble of guessing if they are unaware that you have a guess to make. For example, needing one trick from J 10 opposite K 7 3 2, you should lead the 10. It probably will make no difference, but if left-hand opponent has the ace he is slightly more likely to play it than if you had led the jack, announcing to the world that you have a guess. From his point of view, when you lead the 10, you have a guess only if you hold J 10, and particularly if he is unsure of your length in the suit he may not wish to risk ducking. With no other evidence to the contrary, if he plays low you should play him for the queen. A holding which perhaps lends itself better to this sort of play is A 10 9 3 opposite Q 8 4. If you do not have the entries to take two finesses, you must lead towards the dummy and guess whether to play North for the king or the jack. Left to yourself, it is usually correct to play him for the jack as that also picks up king jack to four. Still, it is a guess, especially if you only need two tricks. If you lead the 10, or the ace followed by the 10, you will put North under pressure. With K x x (x) he will always duck because he can see that you are about to be faced with a choice of plays. If however you lead the 3 first, if will be hard for North to recognize that you have a choice and he may rise with the king. If he does so he has solved your problem, while if he plays low in tempo you should finesse the 8 on the grounds that sometimes he might have played the king if he held it.

King-jack guesses are often just that – guesses. Sometimes you put off the fateful moment as long as possible, hoping to pick up a clue on the way, but all too often, particularly in a high-level contract, there are no clues to be had and you are back to guessing. For this reason, with a holding such as 6 3 opposite K J 4 2 in a slam contract, many players would lead the suit at trick two to pressure North into taking his ace. After all, he might lose it if you had a singleton. Against good defenders this will rarely work. You will often end up with an overtrick when you actually did have a singleton, but you will rarely be spared the fateful guess with a doubleton. Still, if there are no better options available it is worth trying. If North plays low you assume he doesn't have the ace and finesse the jack.

Occasionally you will have a better option available, namely delaying the guess and in the meantime disguising the fact that you have a guess at all.

♠ A Q 10 8 5 2	♠ K J 4 3
♡ A K 10 3	♡ Q J 5
◇ 4	◇ A 6
♣ 6 2	♣ K J 8 3

You are in 6♠ and North leads the king of diamonds. The best shot could be to win and draw trumps, then play four rounds of hearts, pitching dummy's small diamond. Now you lead a club. North knows you have six spades and four hearts, and because you took the trouble to take the diamond discard may assume that you have two diamonds. In that case you only have room for one club, and if he wants to make his ace he must take it now. If he plays low you therefore play him for the queen. This should not really work at teams, where the overtrick is neither here nor there, but at matchpoints it has a fair chance of success, certainly against defenders who do not make a habit of showing their distribution.

In a quite different situation, any time that declarer holds the smallest outstanding spot card, its concealment can cause problems for the defence. If you hold 6 2 opposite K Q 10 7 and want to flush out the ace immediately you should lead the 6 rather than the 2. South will note that the 2 is missing and may assume that his partner has it and has begun a peter. In that case he is much more likely to win the first round and save you a problem later.

Most players, without perhaps knowing the reason, would make the right play in the above example, but very few would in this more subtle situation. You are playing a notrump contract and North leads the 4. Your holding is Q 5 2 opposite 10 6 3. This is a classic situation where if South has A K x he can play either honour and return his small card to give you a guess. If however you conceal the 2 he will not be able to afford that play as you might hold Q x and his partner jack to five. With A K x he will have to cash the other honour, while if he returns a low card you can play low as well, confident that if he has a second honour it will be the jack.

In an attempt to flush out the ace, most players with K Q 10 2 opposite 7 6 5 3 lead low to the king on the first round. Average and weak players will frequently win with the ace when by ducking with A x they could have left the declarer with a nasty guess on the next round. If the king is taken, declarer will finesse the 10 next time, losing only to A J bare. A strong defender, however, will almost invariably duck with A x, leaving you the second-round guess. If he fails to do so it is not unreasonable to assume that it is because he couldn't duck, i.e. he had A or A J bare. Since you would still have a second loser if the suit was 4–1, there is a good case for trying to drop the jack on the second round – but only against a strong defender. Perhaps against him there is a case for changing your initial play and leading to the queen instead of the king. If he does not realize what your holding is he may not bother to duck, again saving you your second-round problem; you will lose only to A J alone.

We have seen how to smoke out an ace; what about a king? With something like A Q J opposite 7 6 3 it is clearly better to finesse the queen first rather than the jack as the queen will be much harder to duck. This principle can be used even when the A Q are in full view on the table.

J 10 5   A Q 9 3

When you lead the jack it is not difficult for South to hold up his king, leaving you in doubt as to its whereabouts. If you want to smoke the king out immediately, try leading low to the queen. This will be much tougher to duck, and if the queen scores it will be reasonable to assume that the king is in the North hand.

♠ Q 5   ♠ A K 9 3
♡ A J 9 6   ♡ K Q
♢ A J 3   ♢ Q 9 8 6
♣ K J 6 5   ♣ A Q 2

The opposition find the safe lead of the 7 of hearts against 7NT, and you see that you have twelve top tricks. The thirteenth can come from the J 10 of spades falling in three rounds, the diamond finesse, or a squeeze. The J 10 of spades are either falling or they are not. Assuming they are not, how are you to decide between the finesse and the squeeze?

You could simply play out all your winners and hope to learn something useful from the opposition's signals, but a far better shot is to win the opening lead in the dummy and immediately lead the queen of diamonds. If South covers your problems are over, while if he plays low without a flicker it is a fair bet that he does not hold the king. In that case you rise with the ace and play to squeeze North in spades and diamonds. If South has managed to play low when holding the king of diamonds he deserves congratulations – he is either a genius or an idiot.

Finally, let's try our hand at finding a queen.

♠ A K 9 7 6 4	♠ J 10 5
♡ K 7	♡ Q J 2
◇ A K Q 10	◇ J 6 3
♣ A	♣ 7 5 3 2

You receive the lead of the queen of clubs against 6♠ and cash a top spade, to which both follow with small cards. The odds just favour playing for the drop, but is there anything better? Suppose you lead the king of hearts next, what will the defence think? They know that you haven't finished drawing trumps yet, so you are unlikely to be trying to set up heart tricks. Not knowing that you already have an entry with the jack of diamonds, they may think you are trying to force a dummy entry to take a trump finesse. Good defenders will let you have a dummy entry only if the finesse is destined to lose, so if they win the ace you should spurn the trump finesse because they obviously want you to take it. If they duck the heart you should assume they are trying to protect South's Q x x of trumps and should cross to the jack of diamonds and run the jack of spades.

Problems for declarer, 17–24

Question No 17

Dealer South   Love all

♠ K 2
♡ A J 10 8 3 2
♢ 10 5
♣ J 6 4

♢ A led

♠ Q 10 9 8 7 6 3
♡ K 4
♢ Q 6
♣ K 5

The bidding

South	West	North	East
3♠[1]	dble[2]	Pass	Pass
Pass			

Final contract – Three Spades doubled

[1] Not everyone's idea of a good three-bid, but this was South's choice at rubber bridge.

[2] In tournament play this double is usually played for take-out, but on the present occasion it was said to be optional – primarily for penalties.

The early play

West cashed two top diamonds and followed with ace and another club.

Preliminary analysis

You have lost three tricks already and the ace of trumps must be classed as a winner for the opposition. The problem seems to be to lose not more than one trick in spades.

Answer No 17

```
                    ♠ K 2
                    ♡ A J 10 8 3 2
                    ♢ 10 5
                    ♣ J 6 4
  ♠ A 5 4                        ♠ J
  ♡ Q 7                          ♡ 9 6 5
  ♢ A K 9 3 2                    ♢ J 8 7 4
  ♣ A 7 3                        ♣ Q 10 9 8 2
                    ♠ Q 10 9 8 7 6 3
                    ♡ K 4
                    ♢ Q 6
                    ♣ K 5
```

South opens three spades, West doubles for penalties, and all pass. West begins with the top diamonds, followed by ace and another club.

You may think that West probably holds something like A J x of spades, but it is not certain. Four top winners would be enough for his double of three spades.

Is there any way in which you can improve your chance of holding the trump loss to one trick? Maybe you can form a plan that may lead West into an indiscretion.

First, play the jack of clubs from dummy; this will be covered by the queen and king. Cash the king of hearts, then lead the 6 of spades.

West may think that you are going to pitch a losing club on the ace of hearts. If he has A J x of trumps he will no doubt play small in the hope of making two spade tricks; if he does so, you intend to run the 6. But with A x or A x x of spades West will surely rise with the ace, hoping to cash a club before you have obtained a (possible) discard on the ace of hearts. He will be sadly disappointed, but you can live with that, no doubt.

Dealer South   Game all

♠ K 7 2
♡ 10 4 2
◇ A 6 3
♣ A J 7 5

◇ J led

♠ A J 3
♡ A 8 7 6 3
◇ K Q 7
♣ Q 4

The bidding

South	West	North	East
1 ♡	Pass	2 ♣	Pass
2 NT	Pass	3 ♡[1]	Pass
4 ♡	Pass	Pass	Pass

Final contract – Four Hearts

[1] There was a long debate in the *Bridge World* some years ago as to whether North in this kind of sequence should raise to 3NT or should bid Three Hearts (forcing) to give partner a choice. It is easy to construct hands where either course would be successful. I must say I would always raise in notrumps.

The early play

West leads the jack of diamonds, which you can win in either hand.

Preliminary analysis

The obvious losers are two, possibly three, trumps and possibly one trick in the black suits; not two, because if the club finesse loses you will have a discard for the third spade.

Answer No 18

```
                    ♠ K 7 2
                    ♡ 10 4 2
                    ◇ A 6 3
                    ♣ A J 7 5
♠ Q 10 8 6 5                      ♠ 9 4
♡ J                              ♡ K Q 9 5
◇ J 10 9 5                        ◇ 8 4 2
♣ 8 6 2                          ♣ K 10 9 3
                    ♠ A J 3
                    ♡ A 8 7 6 3
                    ◇ K Q 7
                    ♣ Q 4
```

South	West	North	East
1 ♡	Pass	2 ♣	Pass
2 NT	Pass	3 ♡	Pass
4 ♡	Pass	Pass	Pass

West leads the jack of diamonds. This is an occasion where the psychological play is also the best technical play. You should win the opening lead in dummy and advance the 10 of hearts. This will save a trick by force when West has the bare 9 and will often gain when East covers with K Q 9 5, K J 9 5, or Q J 9 5.

If on this occasion East covers the 10 of hearts with the queen you win and return the 8 of hearts to his 9. If East attacks spades now, it is probably right to win with the ace and take the club finesse. You have a good chance to make the contract for the loss of two hearts and one club.

There are many situations where the defenders may be trapped into an unwise cover. For example:

J 6

A 8 7 4 3 2

Here the jack from dummy cannot cost a trick; it gains by force
when West holds a singleton 9, perhaps by stealth when East
holds K 10 9 x or Q 10 9 x.

Dealer East   Love all
- ♠ Q J 3
- ♡ Q 7 3 2
- ♢ 7 6
- ♣ A Q 10 5

♡ J led

- ♠ K 10 9 7 4
- ♡ 5
- ♢ K 10 5
- ♣ K J 8 4

The bidding

South	West	North	East
—	—	—	1 ♡
1 ♠	2 ♡	3 ♠	Pass
4 ♠	Pass	Pass	Pass

Final contract – Four Spades

The early play

West leads the jack of hearts, which holds the trick. He switches to a low trump, won by dummy's queen. A diamond is covered by the jack and the king wins. East takes the diamond return and leads a second round of trumps. West wins with the ace of spades and plays a third round.

Preliminary analysis

You have lost three tricks already and the accurate defence has left you with a losing diamond and no trump remaining in dummy. Is there any way in which you may possibly be able to avoid losing another trick?

Answer No 19

```
                    ♠ Q J 3
                    ♡ Q 7 3 2
                    ◇ 7 6
                    ♣ A Q 10 5
   ♠ A 8 2                          ♠ 6 5
   ♡ J 10 4                         ♡ A K 9 8 6
   ◇ 9 8 4 3 2                      ◇ A Q J
   ♣ 7 3                            ♣ 9 6 2
                    ♠ K 10 9 7 4
                    ♡ 5
                    ◇ K 10 5
                    ♣ K J 8 4
```

South	West	North	East
—	—	—	1 ♡
1 ♠	2 ♡	3 ♠	Pass
4 ♠	Pass	Pass	Pass

West leads the jack of hearts and switches to a low trump, won in dummy. East wins the second round of diamonds and returns a trump, West playing ace and another.

South appears to have no way of avoiding the loss of the third round of diamonds, but there is a slight possibility nevertheless. Win the third spade in dummy and ruff a heart. Play the 8 of clubs to the ace and ruff another heart. Now the king of clubs, playing the 10 from dummy, the jack of clubs to the queen and, at trick 12, the 5 of clubs from the table. East is down to ace of hearts and queen of diamonds. It is just possible – no, it is quite likely – that he won't know whether dummy's 5 of clubs is a master or not. You may well achieve the prettiest form of pseudo-squeeze.

Question No 20

Dealer South   E–W vulnerable
♠ Q 8 5 2
♡ A J 7 3
♢ 10 6 2
♣ 7 4

♠ K led
♠ 10 6 3
♡ K Q 10 8 4
♢ A Q
♣ A K 5

The bidding

South	West	North	East
1 ♡	1 ♠	2 ♡	Pass
4 ♡	Pass	Pass	Pass

Final contract – Four Hearts

The early play

West leads the king of spades, low from dummy, the 4 from East.

Preliminary analysis

The diamond finesse is probably wrong, and if West continues with ace and jack of spades, East ruffing the queen, you are likely to go down. What is the best counter-measure?

```
                    ♠ Q 8 5 2
                    ♡ A J 7 3
                    ◇ 10 6 2
                    ♣ 7 4
♠ A K J 9 7                        ♠ 4
♡ 9 2                              ♡ 6 5
◇ K J 5                            ◇ 9 8 7 4 3
♣ Q 6 2                            ♣ J 10 9 8 3
                    ♠ 10 6 3
                    ♡ K Q 10 8 4
                    ◇ A Q
                    ♣ A K 5
```

South	West	North	East
1 ♡	1 ♠	2 ♡	Pass
4 ♡	Pass	Pass	Pass

West leads the king of spades and East plays the 4. There is an obvious danger that you may lose three spades and a diamond.

There is only a small point here, but it turns up quite often and the declarer must know in advance what he is going to do. Most players in South's position would drop the 6 or 10. West will then know that his partner is short, because East would not be playing the 4 from 10 4 3 or 6 4 3. So the 3 is declarer's best play.

There are many situations of this sort and unfortunately it is not safe to rely on general rules. Before playing from dummy you have to reflect on the best way to deceive an opponent.

```
              Q J 8 2
6 led                      A K 10 9 5 3
              7 4
```

West leads the 6 and the jack is covered by the king. Now play the 7, because from East's point of view it might not be good play to continue the suit if his partner held a doubleton. The 7 would also be right if you held 7 4 3.

Question No 21

Dealer East   Love all

♠ J 10 8 6 4
♡ 7 6
♢ 9 7 2
♣ 6 3 2

♢ 6 led

♠ K Q 9 7
♡ A 5 2
♢ A Q 3
♣ A 10 5

The bidding

South	West	North	East
—	—	—	1♠
dble	Pass	2♣	Pass
2NT	Pass	Pass	Pass

Final contract – 2NT

The early play

West leads a low diamond to the jack and queen.

Preliminary analysis

Seven tricks are easily in sight, but no more, apparently, because East has opened one spade and will doubtless hold up the ace.

```
                    ♠ J 10 8 6 4
                    ♡ 7 6
                    ◇ 9 7 2
                    ♣ 6 3 2
♠ —                                 ♠ A 5 3 2
♡ J 9 8 4                           ♡ K Q 10 3
◇ K 10 8 6 4                        ◇ J 5
♣ Q 9 8 4                           ♣ K J 7
                    ♠ K Q 9 7
                    ♡ A 5 2
                    ◇ A Q 3
                    ♣ A 10 5
```

South	West	North	East
—	—	—	1♠
dble	Pass	2♣	Pass
2NT	Pass	Pass	Pass

West leads a low diamond to the jack and queen. South can see seven tricks, but maybe no more, because when East sees his partner show out in spades he will surely hold up the ace.

This was a famous hand in its day, and if you are an assiduous reader of bridge literature you may have seen it before. If so, you won't mind seeing it again, and if not, pause for a while and see if you can find the same play as the great American expert, Howard Schenken.

I will give you a hint: the key to effective deception is the ability to put yourself in a defender's place and think as he does. Knowing what he is likely to do, you play to enlist his aid.

Have you thought of anything clever? No? At trick two Schenken returned a low diamond. West won and played a third round. What more natural now than for East to part with one of his spades?

Dealer South   N–S vulnerable

♠ 7 5 2
♡ 7
♢ J 9 6 4 3
♣ J 7 4 2

♡ 3 led

♠ A K Q
♡ A K 6
♢ K 5 2
♣ K Q 10 5

The bidding

South	West	North	East
2♣	Pass	2♢	Pass
2NT[1]	Pass	3NT[2]	Pass
Pass	Pass		

Final contract – 3NT

[1] Acol-type, usually 23–24 points, non-forcing.
[2] It is the sort of hand that will usually produce seven or nine tricks, depending on whether the diamonds can be brought in.

The early play

West leads the 3 of hearts and East plays the jack.

Preliminary analysis

The diamond situation is not favourable, in the sense that the suit cannot be established for just one loser. Without the diamonds there seem to be only eight tricks. The first question is whether or not to win the first heart.

                    ♠ 7 5 2
                    ♡ 7
                    ◇ J 9 6 4 3
                    ♣ J 7 4 2

♠ 10 9 3   ♠ J 8 6 4
♡ Q 10 8 3 2   ♡ J 9 5 4
◇ Q 8   ◇ A 10 7
♣ A 9 3   ♣ 8 6

                    ♠ A K Q
                    ♡ A K 6
                    ◇ K 5 2
                    ♣ K Q 10 5

South	West	North	East
2♣	Pass	2◇	Pass
2NT	Pass	3NT	Pass
Pass	Pass		

West leads the 3 of hearts and East plays the jack. You know the hearts are 5–4 and there is no point in holding up, allowing the defenders to count the suit on the next lead.

If you play on clubs you will establish eight tricks, but will have no time to arrive at a ninth. The best play is lay down the king of diamonds at trick two. It will be quite difficult for East, as the cards lie, to take the ace at once. If he ducks, then of course you will turn to clubs

This is one of the deceptive plays that is well known but must always stand a chance of success. Much depends, as always, on the tempo of declarer's play. It is no use, obviously, to capture the first heart, do some counting, and then produce the king of diamonds.

Question No 23

Dealer South   Love all

♠ 9 7 5 2
♡ Q 7 4
◇ K J 4
♣ K Q 6

♠ 6 led

♠ K J 4
♡ 10 6 3
◇ A 10 8 5 2
♣ A J

The bidding

South	West	North	East
1NT	Pass	2NT	Pass
3NT	Pass	Pass	Pass

Final contract – 3NT

The early play

West leads the 6 of spades and East plays the 10.

Preliminary analysis

If you can make five tricks in diamonds you will be home. If you fail to find the queen you will be in danger, obviously, of losing several tricks in the major suits.

125

```
                    ♠ 9 7 5 2
                    ♡ Q 7 4
                    ◇ K J 4
                    ♣ K Q 6
   ♠ A Q 8 6 3                    ♠ 10
   ♡ A 5 2                        ♡ K J 9 8
   ◇ Q 6                          ◇ 9 7 3
   ♣ 9 5 3                        ♣ 10 8 7 4 2
                    ♠ K J 4
                    ♡ 10 6 3
                    ◇ A 10 8 5 2
                    ♣ A J
```

South	West	North	East
1NT	Pass	2NT	Pass
3NT	Pass	Pass	Pass

West leads the 6 of spades to East's 10.

There will be nine tricks if South can pick up the diamonds without loss, but life is not like that, so he must consider what chance he may have if the diamond finesse loses.

A clever sequence of play will make him a strong favourite. Win the first trick with the *king* of spades, cross to the king of diamonds and run the jack. If this loses, then certainly West, placing his partner with the jack of spades – presumably J 10 doubleton – will be disposed to lead a low spade. Indeed, he will learnedly select the 8, to point the fact that his re-entry is in hearts. But alas, it will be too late.

This play of the king of spades is less well known than the deceptive play in the following situation:

```
            7 4 2
K Q 10 6 5                    8 3
            A J 9
```

On the lead of the king South drops the jack. This may encourage West to lead a second round when a switch to another suit would be better for the defence.

Question No 24

Dealer South   Game all

    ♠ 6 5 2
    ♡ K 8 4 3
    ◇ 7 3
    ♣ 8 7 4 2

D J led   ◇ J led

    ♠ A K J 4
    ♡ A Q 7
    ◇ A Q
    ♣ Q J 10 3

The bidding

South	West	North	East
2♣	Pass	2◇	Pass
2NT	Pass	3♣	Pass
3♠	Pass	3NT	Pass
Pass	Pass		

Final contract – 3NT

The early play

West's lead of the jack of diamonds runs to the declarer's queen.

Preliminary analysis

South sees that he will not have time to develop the clubs, as this will surely enable the defenders to take two clubs and at least three diamonds.

There are several ways in which the major suits may provide seven tricks. What is the best way to set about the play?

```
                    ♠ 6 5 2
                    ♡ K 8 4 3
                    ◇ 7 3
                    ♣ 8 7 4 2
    ♠ Q 8                          ♠ 10 9 7 3
    ♡ 10 6 2                       ♡ J 9 5
    ◇ J 10 9 8 4                   ◇ K 6 5 2
    ♣ A 9 5                        ♣ K 6
                    ♠ A K J 4
                    ♡ A Q 7
                    ◇ A Q
                    ♣ Q J 10 3
```

South	West	North	East
2♣	Pass	2◇	Pass
2NT	Pass	3♣	Pass
3♠	Pass	3NT	Pass
Pass	Pass		

West leads the jack of diamonds and East plays the 6, as he does not expect his partner to hold A J 10.

You need to develop seven tricks in the majors, and if you begin with ace, queen and another heart you will still need to make three tricks in spades.

There is a slightly better play, not at all obvious. Begin the hearts by leading the *queen*. A defender who holds three small or a doubleton will surely want to give his partner the count, in case partner holds A x x or similar.

You begin with queen and ace of hearts, therefore. Then, if you have formed the conclusion that you are going to make four tricks in hearts, you make the safety play for three tricks in spades. You cash the ace and king, which, as I am sure you know, provides the extra chance for three tricks when West holds Q x.

If you form the opinion that the hearts are not going to break, then you will attempt to win four tricks in spades, taking the normal finesse.

7

Make them guess

The other side of the coin to avoiding a tricky guess oneself is to make the opposition guess. Sometimes this can be merely a question of keeping one defender in the dark as to who holds a particular card, sometimes you may paint a false picture and give him a guess on which the fate of the whole hand will depend. Indeed, that is all we have been doing throughout this book, transferring our problems to the opposition.

If a side suit is distributed A 10 2 opposite 9 6 4 and the opening lead is the queen, the normal play is to duck. Fine, but why not drop the 10? North may switch, seeing no point in continuing the suit if his partner holds the missing 2. Even if he does continue there may be some subsequent confusion as to the whereabouts of the 2, and confusion can only be beneficial to your cause.

Holding A K 9 opposite 10 5 3, when North leads a low card it is all too easy to play low from the dummy without even thinking. By now you should be getting the idea that it is worth thinking before making these automatic plays, and here is a case in point. If you play low and South is forced to play the jack or queen, North will know immediately that you hold the 9, so will not lead the suit a second time. If dummy's 10 forces the jack or queen he is in the dark about the 9 and may lead them again, presenting you with three tricks. How, after all, would you have played with A K 2?

Perhaps you have a trump holding of A Q 10 9 5 opposite 7 3 2, with which you would normally take two finesses, but unfortunately you have no dummy entry so are obliged to play the suit from hand. When you cash the ace and no honour appears it will probably be a pure guess whether to play for doubleton king or doubleton jack. There is a reason to continue with the queen in these circumstances, however. If you lead the 10 and it loses to the jack, the defenders will both have a pretty fair idea that they have another trump trick to come. If instead you lead the queen and the jack doesn't drop, only one defender knows the true position, and as always the less a defender knows about the hand the better the chance that he will make a mistake.

Just consistently playing the right card may make life more difficult for the defence even when that card in no way improves your chances of actually winning the trick. An obvious example is where you hold something like Q 10 9 opposite K 6 2 and North leads the jack. You play low from dummy and, if South takes his ace, drop the queen. You know that the lead is from a short suit, but this way South may think it is from J 10 9 (x). The next example is considerably more subtle.

♠ J 2	♠ K 10 8 5
♡ A Q 10 9 6 5 3	♡ K J 2
◇ —	◇ A K 8
♣ A J 8 2	♣ K 10 4

East opens 1NT (15–17) and feeling in scientific mood you leap straight to 6♡. Not surprisingly, North takes a little time to find a lead; eventually he emerges with the 3 of spades. How do you play? On the auction North might certainly consider underleading an ace, but the odds must surely favour playing him for the queen. Either that will be right or it will be wrong, but is there any hope if he has underled the ace? South will not be aware of the true position, though he will be aware of the possibilities. The trick is to play as though you held A x (x), giving South an awkward decision if he holds the 9 as well as the queen. With A x (x) you would undoubtedly play the 8 from dummy, so that is also the right play with your actual holding. If South has Q 9 x he will be very tempted to put in the 9, in which case you will survive your misguess. If you had played a lazy small card from the dummy he might have wondered why you failed to play the 'normal' card and would have been more likely to play his queen. If South does play the queen you should of course drop the jack. It will probably make no difference, but you never know – opponents have been known to switch.

Playing similar holdings in identical fashions can cause the defence some very awkward moments. How are they to tell which holding you actually have?

(1) A J 9   K 10 2

(2) J 7 3   K 10 2

If you tackle both these holdings by leading the jack first you are bound to benefit some of the time. North may cover in (1) or fail to cover in (2). If you have the first holding and he does play low, your best bet will be to play the king and finesse on the way back. Had North held the queen, some of the time he would have covered the jack.

Similarly, you should lead the 10 with either of these holdings:

(3) 10 7 3   A J 5

(4) K 10 9   A J 5

North leads low and you hold:

(5) A J   Q 10 3

(6) A J 4   Q 10 2

With (5) play the queen; South may cover. With (6) play the queen and, if this is not covered, drop the jack! North may lead the suit again, thinking you had A J alone.

135

You must surely gain some of the time from the pressure you put on North, and similarly in this example:

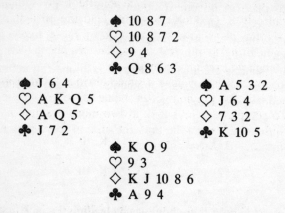

♠ 10 8 7
♡ 10 8 7 2
♢ 9 4
♣ Q 8 6 3

♠ J 6 4
♡ A K Q 5
♢ A Q 5
♣ J 7 2

♠ A 5 3 2
♡ J 6 4
♢ 7 3 2
♣ K 10 5

♠ K Q 9
♡ 9 3
♢ K J 10 8 6
♣ A 9 4

South opens 1♢ and you reach 3NT, North leading the 9 of diamonds. Easily the best chance of a ninth trick is to lead the jack of clubs early in the play. How can North, who probably has the greater length in the suit, tell what is going on? Except perhaps when he also holds the 9, he will rarely cover with the queen. If you have the ace, he expects to make his queen as you are likely to play the opening bidder for the points.

As we have already seen, one's chances of setting up a long suit can often be improved by ducking the first round. We examined earlier the possibility of leading low from dummy with 6 3 opposite A Q 7 4 2; similarly, if it is not convenient to cross to hand to lead the first round, try leading low from dummy's suit with such as 6 3 opposite A K 10 5 4. You may catch South going in with Q x or even Q x x x. True, in the first case you have to decide whether or not to finesse on the next round – you will look silly if South has Q J or Q J x – but the tempo of his play should provide a clue. If he thinks and then plays the queen he surely does not have the jack as well.

One of the joys of playing weak two bids is that occasionally one has to play a trump suit like A J 10 6 4 2 opposite a void. The legitimate chance of only losing two trump tricks is to lead ace and a low one, succeeding whenever either defender has K Q or K Q x. A better shot, which admittedly gives up on the rather unlikely K Q doubleton, is to lead the 10 first. If an unwary North plays low from Q x x or more likely from K x x, you bring in the rest of the suit by playing ace and another when you regain the lead.

This chapter does not have a single obvious theme running through it like the previous ones, being more a collection of ideas. To complete it, let's look at two more example hands, totally unrelated except in that the use of psychology can greatly improve declarer's chances.

	♠ J 7 6 4		♠ Q 9
	♡ K 6 4 2		♡ 10 8
	◇ K J 2		◇ 10 9
	♣ J 5		♣ A K Q 10 7 6 3

South	West	North	East
—	—	1◇	3♣
Pass	3 NT	All pass	

North leads a small diamond against your pushy 3NT. Perhaps partner would have been better advised to overcall a simple 2♣. It looks as though South probably has at least one high card as otherwise North might have taken further action, and there is a danger of going a lot down if South gets in and leads a diamond through. The best play seems to be to run dummy's clubs immediately, but making five discards is going to be very uncomfortable. Suppose, however, that you overtake dummy's 10 of diamonds with the jack at trick one and then run the clubs. If North is persuaded that you began with K J bare he will probably keep too many diamonds when you run the clubs and you will be able to throw him in at the end to give you a second diamond trick for your contract.

The full deal may be:

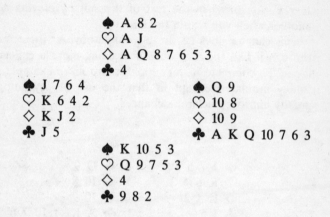

♠ A 8 2
♡ A J
♢ A Q 8 7 6 5 3
♣ 4

♠ J 7 6 4
♡ K 6 4 2
♢ K J 2
♣ J 5

♠ Q 9
♡ 10 8
♢ 10 9
♣ A K Q 10 7 6 3

♠ K 10 5 3
♡ Q 9 7 5 3
♢ 4
♣ 9 8 2

Note how useful it was that your low diamond was lower than South's card, making it look as though he had begun an echo to show a doubleton.

♠ K J
♡ A Q 8 6
♢ A Q J 10 4
♣ K 7

♠ 10 9 7
♡ 5 3
♢ K 9 6
♣ A Q J 10 8

Playing in 6NT (you may have opened 2NT), you receive a passive club lead. On the face of it, you have eleven top tricks and the twelfth can come equally well from any one of three sources – a heart finesse, a spade to the jack, or a spade to the king.

Let's look at those possibilities in turn. If you play a heart to the queen and it loses you have virtually no second chance. If you lead a spade to the jack and it loses to the queen, and North does not hold the ace, there is a fair chance that he will switch, giving you the opportunity to try the heart finesse as well. That gives you two chances, so must be a better shot. Better still, however, is a spade to the king. When North has the ace but not the queen, he is more likely to switch than in the previous case. If you have K Q x he has no wish to present you with a second spade trick at this early stage when you might have an alternative, less successful, option available. In fact, against a good defender the king may score even when the ace is offside. There are two ways in which ducking could gain from North's point of view. If you do hold K Q x (x) you may cross over to dummy and lead a second spade to the queen, while if the king had lost to the ace you would have had no option but to try something else next time. Alternatively, if your hand were slightly different your failure to lose a trick when you wanted to could mean that you would no longer be able to operate a successful squeeze. So a spade to the king, early in the play, can gain in three ways and is the most likely to succeed.

The general principle also holds good in lower level contracts. With a choice of leading to a king or an A Q, it may look safer to try the latter first, but in practice that is not so, as the average defender will find it hard to believe that you would lead to an unsupported king when you had a reasonable alternative. Even when the ace proves to be wrong they will often switch to another suit.

Reading the signals

A large number of the deceptive plays we have looked at have depended on misleading the defence about our distribution in a particular suit. Defenders who slavishly show their distribution should therefore be able to overcome many of our efforts. That is quite true, and often they do realize what we are trying to do, though by no means as often as they might. Perhaps they don't altogether trust their partners; or perhaps they belong to the old-fashioned school that doesn't believe in regular signalling by the defenders. Accurate signalling does make the defence easier, but it has its disadvantages too, and we must consider now how the declarer should play against conventional defenders. First, he may try to confuse their signals, making them as hard as possible to read, and second he may profit from the information supplied by the signals.

We have already seen that if the opening lead is an honour we should generally signal as though we were a defender, i.e. play a high spot card if we want the suit continued, a low one if we want a switch. We can interfere with length signals as well, though not quite in the same way. Usually this will simply entail concealing the lowest card in the suit.

(1) Q 4 2   A K 7

(2) K 5 2   A Q J 4

In each case North leads the 8 and we win with the ace and the queen respectively. Against a pair who play distributional signals, if South follows with the 3 we know immediately that he

140

has an odd number, probably three. This information is useful in itself, particularly when this is a side suit in a trump contract as it helps us to decide how many rounds of the suit we can afford to play without drawing trumps. It also helps us to build up a picture of the distribution of the opposing hands so that often after three or four tricks we know both defenders' exact shapes.

While our little subterfuge may not survive the next round of the suit, it may be worth playing the 4 in (1) and the 5 in (2). North cannot be sure that his partner has not started an echo, so he often gains no information from the length signal – only you do. Note the value of holding the 2, or the 3 if dummy has the 2. When the spot card you conceal is the smallest outstanding card you can be certain of creating doubt in at least one defender's mind.

Entryless dummy situations, where the defence has to decide when to take the ace of dummy's long suit, lend themselves perfectly to this sort of play.

(1) J 6 2   K Q 10 9

(2) J 6   K Q 10 9

With no side entry the best play depends on which defender you think is more likely to hold the ace. In either case you start by leading the jack. If you think North is more likely to hold the ace, you should allow the jack to hold and next lead the 6, concealing the 2. North, with A x x, may think his partner has begun an echo and take his ace a round too soon, enabling you to make a total of three tricks from the suit. After all, if you had J 6 doubleton he would be right to take the ace. When you think it is South who holds the ace you must overtake the jack in dummy so that when you lead the second round he has to make his play without the benefit of seeing his partner's second card. He may duck again when he holds A x x or A x x x.

Now you cannot conceal anything from North so must base your play on the assumption that it is South who holds the ace. In that case leading the 3 to dummy and continuing with dummy's second honour will leave him guessing the whereabouts of the 2. Usually he will duck just in case.

So the principles to remember are to conceal the lowest card and to arrange to lead the second round through the defender you think has the ace. That combination creates a guessing situation; nothing else does.

Often you can use the opposition's signals to solve your own problems. It is true that this can be risky as good defenders will do their best to mislead you if they are aware of the point of the hand, but early in the play most defenders can be relied on to stay honest most of the time. Declarer did well to make 4♠ on this board from a pairs event:

```
        ♠ A Q 10 8 7 5 4    ♠ —
        ♡ —                 ♡ Q 9 8 5 3
        ◇ A J 3             ◇ K 7 4
        ♣ 10 6 4            ♣ A Q 7 3 2
```

South	West	North	East
1◇	4♠	All pass	

The opening lead was the 6 of diamonds to South's queen, and declarer started well by leading the 7 of spades at trick two. This ran round to South's king and the return of diamond 2 was ruffed by North. A heart to South's ace was ruffed and declarer drew trumps, North having started with J 9 x x. Declarer's problem was how to play the club suit for only one loser. Should he finesse or play to drop the doubleton king? There was certainly room for North to hold the king of clubs as South would doubtless have played the ace of hearts from A K. But, declarer had no doubts. He cashed the ace of clubs, ruffed a heart, and played a low club, ducking when North played the 9. When the king fell he had made his contract for an excellent score.

Why was declarer so confident? The diamond 2 that South led at trick three to give his partner a ruff was an obvious suit preference signal, so he was marked with the king of clubs.

Sometimes you may have to work a shade harder to obtain the information you want. Take this 3NT hand:

♠ A Q 4	♠ 7 5 3 2
♡ A Q 5	♡ 7 3
♢ A Q J 9	♢ K 8 6 4
♣ A Q 7	♣ 6 5 3

South	West	North	East
—	—	2♡ (6–10)	Pass
Pass	dble	Pass	2♠
Pass	3NT	Pass	Pass

North leads the 6 of hearts to South's 10, giving you your eighth trick. Either black queen could be the ninth, but with only one dummy entry you can take only one finesse. Which should it be? A studious West might cash the ace of spades – singleton kings do appear sometimes. But there is a better plan.

At trick two you should return a low heart! North will win and no doubt clear the suit, but will he not signal his entry to his partner in the process? With the king of spades he will return a high heart, while with the king of clubs he will play a low heart. Obviously you take your finesse in the suit he doesn't advertise.

143

The declarer may profit equally from the enemy's length signals. Say you open 2NT and dummy goes down with K 10 x x in spades and nothing else. Fortunately you hold A Q x in spades, so the suit will provide three or four tricks, but you could still be faced with an awkward guess on the third round. Try leading the queen at your first opportunity and you will probably get an honest count signal, resolving your guess for you. If on the other hand you lead the ace first the defenders will have no reason to signal. When the queen is led they will be eager to help one another.

The same sort of idea can be used to improve your chances of a winning decision in this slam:

♠ A K 7	♠ Q 6 4 2
♡ A K Q 5	♡ J 7
♢ A Q J 4	♢ K 3 2
♣ 9 6	♣ K 7 5 2

You are in 6NT on the lead of 10 of hearts, and you have eleven tricks. The twelfth can come either from a 3–3 spade break or finding the ace of clubs onside. The trouble is that you cannot afford to try the spades first in case North has four along with his club ace. If you win the jack of hearts and play a spade to the ace, however, you are likely to get an honest count signal from at least one defender.

Now, suppose one defender plays low while the other starts an echo. It could be simply that someone has a doubleton honour and cannot afford to show distribution. The other possibility is that one of them is trying to fool you by giving a false count. You can test their honesty by next playing a diamond to the king. Watch their diamond signals and when you cash out the rest of the diamonds you will discover who has been honest and who has not. As the defenders cannot know which is the critical suit so early in the play, they are likely to be honest on both occasions or, less likely, dishonest. If you see which defender you can trust in diamonds, you will get a good idea which one you can trust in the critical suit, spades. You will base your play accordingly.

This last paragraph assumes that you are playing against defenders who habitually signal in these positions. Bad players – and some good players – do not.

One more slam to finish with:

♠ A K	♠ J 7 3 2
♡ Q 7 3 2	♡ A
◇ A K Q J 4	◇ 10 6 5 3
♣ K 9	♣ A Q J 4

Tempted by the lure of a matchpoint top, you shoot 7NT rather than settle for the cold 7◇. Alas, there are only twelve top tricks, but fortunately there is a chance of a thirteenth as the hand reduces to:

♠ K	♠ J 7
♡ Q 7	♡ A
◇ —	◇ —
♣ —	♣ —

If either defender began with both the spade queen and heart king you have him well and truly squeezed. The only problem, as with many squeeze endings, is that you may not be sure which honour he has unguarded. However, the defensive signalling should provide a clue. The defender with the key cards will not have done much signalling. He can see that signals can be of no use to his partner and is not going to give you any free information. His partner, on the other hand, will be doing everything he can to help and is likely to be honest in his discards. If you can work out which defender has been under

145

pressure and then trust his *partner's* signals, you will have a very good chance of getting the ending right.

Though it is not within the scope of this book, I may add that many successful squeezes are brought off for precisely this reason. The player with all the high cards frequently knows all he needs to know about the hand without any help from his partner and all that signalling does is draw a blueprint of the hand for declarer. Unless playing against opponents whom you know to be extremely devious, I advise you to trust their signals to solve your guesses, whether in a squeeze situation or simply whether a suit is breaking or not. Most players need their partner's help, especially against such a fine deceptive player as yourself, so they will generally signal honestly. Certainly you will be unlucky to find them both false-carding at the same moment. But I admit there is another type. Some defenders, aware of your skill, will abandon their normal habits and false-card all over the place. Just observe what they do – and never comment on it.

Question No 25

Dealer South   Love all

```
                    ♠ J 6 3 2
                    ♡ A Q 7 2
                    ◇ 8 2
                    ♣ A K 10
♠ A K 5
♡ 9                    ┌─────────┐
◇ A Q J 9 7 3          │    N    │
♣ Q 4 2                │ W     E │
                       │    S    │
                       └─────────┘
```

The bidding

South	West	North	East
2♡[1]	3◇	4♡	Pass
Pass	Pass		

Final contract – Four Hearts

[1] Weak, normally 6–10

The early play

You lead three rounds of spades, declarer turning up with Q 8 and discarding a diamond on the jack. South ruffs the last spade with ♡ 10 and plays two rounds of trumps, East following. South continues with ace and king of clubs, discarding another diamond, then ruffs the 10 of clubs and leads the 10 of diamonds.

Preliminary analysis

You need to make two more tricks to defeat the contract. Is it so easy?

```
                        ♠ J 6 3 2
                        ♡ A Q 7 2
                        ◇ 8 2
                        ♣ A K 10
      ♠ A K 5                           ♠ 10 9 7 4
      ♡ 9                               ♡ 5 3
      ◇ A Q J 9 7 3                     ◇ K
      ♣ Q 4 2                           ♣ J 9 8 6 5 3
                        ♠ Q 8
                        ♡ K J 10 8 6 4
                        ◇ 10 6 5 4
                        ♣ 7
```

South	West	North	East
2♡	3◇	4♡	Pass
Pass	Pass		

You began with three rounds of spades, declarer discarding a diamond on the jack. He ruffs the last spade high, draws trumps, and plays three rounds of clubs, discarding another diamond and ruffing the third round. Then he leads ◇ 10 from hand.

You know that declarer is 2–6–4–1, so you confidently play the jack of diamonds on the 10 and cash the ace. Wait a minute! If declarer has four diamonds, that leaves partner with a singleton. What if it is the king? He will be forced to overtake the jack and concede a ruff-and-discard. You can guard against this by rising with the ace (a Crocodile Coup), swallowing partner's king.

Well played all round, but a very good declarer might play exactly the same way with K 10 x x of diamonds – playing for a phantom crocodile. If he brings it off he'll have a story to tell.

Have you any indication? Perhaps partner, with a low singleton in diamonds, might have thought of discarding downwards in clubs, to warn you not to rely on him for a diamond honour. But that's not very strong, I agree. If South has made this play with ♢ K 10 x x, you must give credit where credit is due.

Question No 26

Dealer North   Game all

```
                    ♠ Q 10 8 6 2
                    ♡ A J 8 4 3
                    ◇ 4
                    ♣ A K
    ♠ A 4          ┌─────────────┐
    ♡ K 10 5 2     │      N      │
    ◇ Q 7 3 2      │  W       E  │
    ♣ 7 5 2        │      S      │
                   └─────────────┘
```

The bidding

South	West	North	East
—	—	1♠	Pass
2♣	Pass	2♡	Pass
2NT	Pass	3NT	Pass
Pass	Pass		

Final contract – 3NT

The early play

Your low diamond lead goes to the king and 10. Partner returns
◇5, declarer playing the jack. What now?

Preliminary analysis

South can hardly have A J 10 alone, or he would have cap-
tured the first trick. J 10 9 8, perhaps? In that case you can
lead a diamond to partner's ace and then play against the
dummy, as it were. Is that how you see it?

Answer No 26

```
                    ♠ Q 10 8 6 2
                    ♡ A J 8 4 3
                    ◇ 4
                    ♣ A K
♠ A 4                                   ♠ K J 9 5
♡ K 10 5 2                              ♡ Q 9 6
◇ Q 7 3 2                               ◇ K 9 6 5
♣ 7 5 2                                 ♣ 8 3
                    ♠ 7 3
                    ♡ 7
                    ◇ A J 10 8
                    ♣ Q J 10 9 6 4
```

South	West	North	East
—	—	1♠	Pass
2♣	Pass	2♡	Pass
2NT	Pass	3NT	Pass
Pass	Pass		

A low diamond lead went to the king and 10. East returned ◇5, declarer playing the jack and West the queen.

It seems possible that declarer is making a rather clumsy attempt to disguise a holding of J 10 9 8. If that is the case, we can lead a diamond to partner's ace and he will exit with a club.

But cashing partner's ace of diamonds will keep – a club switch at trick three will be just as effective. More to the point, if the deal is as shown a third diamond will prove fatal: South will dispose of dummy's A K of clubs and run nine tricks.

Declarer's imaginative play deserves some reward, but his 2NT (instead of a cautious 2♠) was optimistic, was it not?

154

Question No 27

Dealer South   Game all

♠ A J 10 7 3
♡ Q 6 3
◇ Q J 3
♣ 5 2

♣ A led

```
      N
  W       E
      S
```

♠ Q 8 2
♡ K J 9
◇ K 8 7
♣ 10 6 4 3

The bidding

South	West	North	East
1♡	2♣	2♠	3♣
3♡	4♣	4♡	Pass
Pass	Pass		

Final contract – Four Hearts

The early play

Partner leads the ace of clubs, bringing down declarer's king, and switches to the diamond 10, which is covered by the queen, king and ace. A spade goes to the 10 and queen, you return a diamond to dummy's jack, and declarer plays the heart queen from dummy.

Preliminary analysis

To cover the queen of hearts with the king would be a disaster if partner held the singleton ace. Is that possible? Hardly; South must have better than six to the 10. Do you want to give South a tempo by not covering the queen? It seems natural to cover.

```
                    ♠ A J 10 7 3
                    ♡ Q 6 3
                    ◇ Q J 3
                    ♣ 5 2
  ♠ K 9 4                         ♠ Q 8 2
  ♡ —                             ♡ K J 9
  ◇ 10 9 6 2                      ◇ K 8 7
  ♣ A Q J 9 8 7                   ♣ 10 6 4 3
                    ♠ 6 5
                    ♡ A 10 8 7 5 4 2
                    ◇ A 5 4
                    ♣ K
```

South	West	North	East
1♡	2♣	2♠	3♣
3♡	4♣	4♡	Pass
Pass	Pass		

West cashed ♣ A, then led ◇10 to the queen, king and ace. A spade went to the 10 and queen, and you returned a diamond to dummy's jack. Now South led the queen of hearts.

This situation would catch most players at the table. Placing South with the ace of hearts, they would think: Why give him a tempo by playing low? There's a good answer to this: he is evidently planning to win with the ace of hearts and finesse the jack of spades, in the hope of discarding his diamond loser. So you must duck when the queen of hearts is led, and you mustn't think about it, either. If South plays the ace and finesses in spades he will dispose of his diamond but will still be losing four tricks.

Question No 28

Dealer South   E–W vulnerable

♠ 10 8 7 4
♡ A Q 3
♢ J 6 4
♣ K Q 4

♠ Q J 6 2
♡ K 9 6
♢ A Q 10 3
♣ 9 2

♡ 5 led

```
    N
  W   E
    S
```

The bidding

South	West	North	East
1NT	Pass	2NT[1]	Pass
3NT	Pass	Pass	Pass

Final contract – 3NT

[1] You may think that 12 points, including several honour cards, justifies a raise to three. I quite agree, but players are sometimes a little cautious when partner has opened 1NT against vulnerable opponents.

The early play

Partner's lead of the 5 of hearts produces the queen, king and 4.

Preliminary analysis

This play of the queen of hearts on the first trick is a little unusual. Is he afraid of a heart continuation, or does he want it? Perhaps he went in with the queen because he was afraid of a switch to spades or diamonds.

```
                    ♠ 10 8 7 4
                    ♡ A Q 3
                    ♢ J 6 4
                    ♣ K Q 4
    ♠ 9 3                           ♠ Q J 6 2
    ♡ 10 8 7 5 2                    ♡ K 9 6
    ♢ K 7 5                         ♢ A Q 10 3
    ♣ 8 6 3                         ♣ 9 2
                    ♠ A K 5
                    ♡ J 4
                    ♢ 9 8 2
                    ♣ A J 10 7 5
```

South	West	North	East
1NT	Pass	2NT	Pass
3NT	Pass	Pass	Pass

West's lead of the 5 of hearts is covered by the queen and king.

Most players in East's position would return the 9 of hearts, no doubt, but a good defender would think to himself: Why the *queen* of hearts? Declarers usually put in the low card so that the suit will be safe from attack. Maybe he wants me to return a heart because he is wide open in another suit. This suit is much more likely to be diamonds than spades. (If he has only K x of spades, where will nine tricks come from?)

There is a good case for returning a diamond at trick two. But which, the queen or the 3? The 3 would be necessary only if South held 2–2–4–5 distribution. As the cards lie, any diamond switch would be good enough.

Declarer's play of the queen of hearts at trick one was well judged. Two heart tricks were all he needed for game.

Question No 29

Dealer South   Love all

```
            ♠ 10 8 4
            ♡ K 7 3
            ◇ A Q J 8
            ♣ Q J 7
♠ A 6 2      ┌─────────┐
♡ 8 4        │    N    │
◇ 10 7 6 3   │ W     E │
♣ 9 8 5 4    │    S    │
             └─────────┘
```

The bidding

South	West	North	East
2NT	Pass	6NT	Pass
Pass	Pass		

Final contract – 6NT

The early play

You lead a club and dummy's queen holds the trick. Declarer leads a low spade to the king.

Preliminary analysis

An ace can make only once, as some players say, but of course it is not always right to part with an ace on the first round. Another question: If you do play the ace, what will you do next?

Dealer South   Love all

```
                    ♠ 10 8 4
                    ♡ K 7 3
                    ◇ A Q J 8
                    ♣ Q J 7
    ♠ A 6 2                         ♠ J 9 7 3
    ♡ 8 4                           ♡ J 10 9 5
    ◇ 10 7 6 3                      ◇ 9 5
    ♣ 9 8 5 4                       ♣ 10 6 2
                    ♠ K Q 5
                    ♡ A Q 6 2
                    ◇ K 4 2
                    ♣ A K 3
```

South	West	North	East
2NT	Pass	6NT	Pass
Pass	Pass		

West's club lead is won in dummy and declarer plays a spade to the king.

South has done well to play this suit immediately, forcing West to make a decision before he knows much about the hand. As the cards lie, it is essential to hold off. If you win, South will play off his winners in the minor suits and East will be squeezed between the jack of spades and his long hearts. If you duck the spade in good tempo he will probably lead another spade to the queen before playing three rounds of clubs or hearts.

Against the great majority of opponents it would certainly be right to hold off. But a very clever declarer might hold such as:

♠ K 9
♡ A Q J 2
♢ K 9 4 2
♣ A K 3

It is often good tactics to lead towards an unsupported king early in the play, especially when the opponent on your left is a good player. If, in defence, you do decide to win the king with the ace, be sure to return a spade immediately.

Question No 30

Dealer South   Game all

♠ K 8 4 3 2
♡ 9 4 2
◇ Q 7 2
♣ A 10

♡ 6 led

```
      N
   W     E
      S
```

♠ Q 10 6
♡ K 5
◇ K J 9 5
♣ J 7 6 3

The bidding

South	West	North	East
1NT[1]	Pass	3NT[2]	Pass
Pass	Pass		

Final Contract – 3NT

[1] 15–17.
[2] Nothing is more foolish than to show the spades directly or, still worse, to initiate a Stayman sequence. Even if partner has four spades, which is much against the odds, the hand may still play well in notrumps.

The early play

Partner's lead of the 6 of hearts runs to the king and ace. South leads a low club to the 4, 10 and jack.

Preliminary analysis

You have the same sort of problem as on an earlier deal (No. 28). Will you make the obvious return of a heart?

```
                    ♠ K 8 4 3 2
                    ♡ 9 4 2
                    ♢ Q 7 2
                    ♣ A 10
    ♠ J 9 5                         ♠ Q 10 6
    ♡ 10 8 7 6 3                    ♡ K 5
    ♢ A 10 3                        ♢ K J 9 5
    ♣ 9 4                           ♣ J 7 6 3
                    ♠ A 7
                    ♡ A Q J
                    ♢ 8 6 4
                    ♣ K Q 8 5 2
```

South	West	North	East
1NT	Pass	3NT	Pass
Pass	Pass		

West leads the 6 of hearts to the king and ace. Declarer plays a low club to the 10 and jack.

If the clubs were 3–3 South could run nine tricks. However, playing low to the 10 gains when West has J x or (less likely) J x x x, and no doubt the declarer thinks that if the 10 loses to the jack you will hastily return a heart.

But will you? If he were afraid of a heart continuation would South let you have the lead so easily? The most likely explanation is that he has nothing in diamonds and thinks it will be tough for you to switch to a suit where dummy has Q x x. You cannot let him get away with insulting you like this, so switch to a low diamond and show him you are not to be trifled with.

164

Question No 31

Dealer South   E–W vulnerable

```
              ♠ A K
              ♡ 10 9 4 2
              ♢ J 5 2
              ♣ Q 8 6 4
♠ 10 9 7 6 2   ┌─────────┐
♡ K 3          │    N    │
♢ A Q 7        │ W     E │
♣ 9 5 3        │    S    │
               └─────────┘
```

The bidding

South	West	North	East
1♡	Pass	3♡	Pass
4♡	Pass	Pass	Pass

Final contract – Four Hearts

The early play

You lead a spade to dummy's king. Declarer cashes a second round, discarding a club, then runs the 10 of hearts.

Preliminary analysis

You cannot risk holding off, that is certain, because declarer might hold a six-card suit. So you win with the king and must decide whether to return a heart or attack one of the minors.

```
                    ♠ A K
                    ♡ 10 9 4 2
                    ◇ J 5 2
                    ♣ Q 8 6 4
♠ 10 9 7 6 2                        ♠ Q J 8 4 3
♡ K 3                              ♡ 8 5
◇ A Q 7                            ◇ K 8 6
♣ 9 5 3                           ♣ J 10 2
                    ♠ 5
                    ♡ A Q J 7 6
                    ◇ 10 9 4 3
                    ♣ A K 7
```

South	West	North	East
1♡	Pass	3♡	Pass
4♡	Pass	Pass	Pass

West leads a spade to dummy's king. Declarer discards a club on the ace of spades, then runs a heart to West's king.

This is a fairly familiar sort of problem, I agree, but many defenders would still do the wrong thing, attacking clubs because they had seen the declarer discard a club. As the cards lie, this would enable South to discard two diamonds on the Q 8 of clubs.

The point to bear in mind is that South is marked with at most seven cards in the majors, so either six or seven in the minors. There is absolutely no way in which any club trick for the defence can disappear. But a diamond may disappear if South has played a tricky game. To exit with a low diamond is completely safe, because even if declarer has the king partner will be able to lead a second diamond when he comes in with his (possible) club trick.

Question No 32

Dealer North   N–S vulnerable

```
                  ♠ A J 5 3
                  ♡ A Q 3
                  ◇ J 4
                  ♣ A K 6 5
                        ┌─────────┐        ♠ 8
                        │    N    │        ♡ 9 7 6 5
◇ 8 led                 │ W     E │        ◇ K Q 10 7 6
                        │    S    │        ♣ 10 4 3
                        └─────────┘
```

The bidding

South	West	North	East
—	—	1♣	1◇[1]
1♠	Pass	4◇[2]	Pass
4NT	Pass	5♣[3]	Pass
7♠	Pass	Pass	Pass

Final contract – Seven Spades

[1] Overcalls, when not vul against vul, are not to be taken too seriously in match play.

[2] Showing a raise to four spades with good controls.

[3] 0 or 3 aces.

The early play

Partner's 8 of diamonds runs to the 10 and ace. The declarer draws two trumps, then leads the jack of clubs, which is covered by the queen and ace. He plays king and another heart, and discards the 9 of diamonds on the third round. Then he runs four more spades.

Preliminary analysis

Dummy is down to K 6 of clubs and you have to discard from ◇ K and ♣ 10 4. Partner's discards – a heart, a diamond, and two low clubs – have not been particularly helpful. Are you going to throw a diamond or a club?

Answer No 32

```
              ♠ A J 5 3
              ♡ A Q 3
              ◇ J 4
              ♣ A K 6 5
♠ 10 4                        ♠ 8
♡ J 8 4 2                     ♡ 9 7 6 5
◇ 8 2                         ◇ K Q 10 7 6
♣ Q 9 8 7 2                   ♣ 10 4 3
              ♠ K Q 9 7 6 2
              ♡ K 10
              ◇ A 9 5 3
              ♣ J
```

South	West	North	East
—	—	1♣	1◇
1♠	Pass	4◇	Pass
4NT	Pass	5♣	Pass
7♠	Pass	Pass	Pass

West's lead of the 8 of diamonds runs to the 10 and ace. After two rounds of trumps South leads the jack of clubs, which is covered by the queen and ace. Declarer plays three rounds of hearts, discarding ◇ 9, then cashes four more spades.

At the finish East has to discard from ◇ K and ♣ 10 4. In an international match he parted with the king of diamonds and South made the last two tricks with ◇ 5 3.

Partner could have been more helpful, no doubt, but even so there were indications. With 8 5 3 2 of your suit West would probably have led low; and in any case he would have discarded diamonds to give you a count. Still more significant, would South have led ♣ J from J 9 8 at an early stage? So I hope you weren't caught by the declarer's very clever play. It wouldn't be very nice to present the opponents with a grand slam on the last board, would it?